FOCUS ON MURDER

Very few newspapermen go wrong, and if they do, they don't stay newspapermen long. Usually the papers act as their own watchdogs. With Ralph Stacey, though, the Courier *had no suspicions until he was killed. Then they had to know—if possible before the police did.*

Kent Murdock had been on an assignment with Stacey that same night—had been with him when somebody pulled alongside their convertible and blasted two shots through their windshield; had been in his apartment when the girl with the harlequin glasses and the gun walked in; had seen him only hours before somebody put six bullets into him hoodlum-style. Now all he had to find out was who, why, and how.

Here is your favorite news-photographer sleuth back again in a slam-bang story of hate and fear, murder and revenge. George Harmon Coxe, as the New York Times *has said, has long been respected as one of the deans of mystery writing for his "suspenseful mysteries loaded with misdirection and surprises and peopled with likeable and convincing characters." If you haven't read him yet, now's the time to do so.*

GEORGE HARMON COXE

Focus on

Murder

ALFRED · A · KNOPF *NEW YORK*

L. C. CATALOG CARD NUMBER: 54–5262

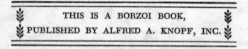

THIS IS A BORZOI BOOK,
PUBLISHED BY ALFRED A. KNOPF, INC.

FOR

JOE LESSER

FOCUS ON MURDER

1

THE MAN was waiting when Kent Murdock came into the Studio—a term used by the employees of the *Courier* to designate the photographic department on the third floor—in the late afternoon of an early spring day.

Sitting near the end of the pipe-rack coat hanger in one of the anteroom's four chairs, he had for some time been staring sightlessly at the bare wall opposite him. Now, seeing Murdock, he glanced at Spencer, who sat behind the community desk reading a paper-backed novel, and Spencer bobbed his head in some silent confirmation as Murdock moved over to the only other desk, a somewhat larger one which was his by right of his job as picture chief.

"Are you the gentleman in charge?"

The visitor was on his feet, hat in hand, a round-faced man in early middle-age, dark-complected and wearing metal-rimmed glasses. He waited as Murdock put down his equipment case and started to shrug out of his balmacaan. When Murdock nodded and said yes, he cleared his throat.

"I'd like to talk to you about a picture."

Murdock sat down, allowed himself a small sigh. He gave Spencer a wry glance and Spencer, sharing the immediate bond of understanding which came to both, shrugged and grinned back at him. For the remark was one which had been frequently heard in one form or another and came as an occupational problem based on the idea that to a newspaper photographer there were only two kinds of people: those who wanted to get their pictures in the paper and those who wanted to keep them out.

"Okay," Murdock said resignedly. "What's it about?"

"Well—there was this accident down on lower Washington Street an hour or so ago. It wasn't much. No one hurt. Just a car up on the sidewalk and people gathered around. I was one of them. I just happened to see it, and right after that this other car drives up and a man gets out with a small camera—a Leica, I think—and takes two quick pictures and then jumps back into the car."

"You think he was from the *Courier*?"

"He said he was. I went over to him as soon as I could and asked if he was a newspaperman, and he said: '*Courier*,' and before I could say anything else he was gone."

Murdock leaned back. "So what's your problem?"

"I was in the picture." The man glanced down at his hat. He twisted the limp brim. "I'm a married man, Mr. Murdock. I—I was with someone I shouldn't have been with. My wife reads the *Courier* and she'll see the picture and I was hoping—"

He let the sentence dangle, but the implication was clear, and while Murdock found nothing wrong with the story he was curious about the man himself. He had noted that the topcoat was threadbare at the collar and wrists, the brown suit beneath it wrinkled and worn. The black hair, missing a butch-cut by an inch, had no part, and the over-all effect was singularly unprepossessing. For all of this he expressed himself like a man who had had a better than average education, and Murdock wondered about this even as he said he thought he understood the problem.

Patiently, because the man seemed sincere, and with no thought of being patronizing, he added that there were some things he should explain. He waved his hand to indicate the sparsely furnished room with its scarred and chipped calcimined walls, the adjacent printing-room, the unseen inner corridor leading to the darkroom cubicles.

"The *Courier*," he said, "maintains this department and a staff to get pictures to print. We take four times as many as ever appear, but the decision as to what will be printed and what won't is made upstairs. We get paid for taking pictures which then become the property of the *Courier*."

"I understand that."

"We don't make decisions here. From what you say I doubt if the picture you refer to is worth any space at all, but that doesn't mean we'd be justified in handing it over to you."

"I understand perfectly. That was not what I had in mind." The man hesitated, continued earnestly. "But the crowd that gathered, including me, is nothing but background. It's unimportant certainly, and I understand you retouch photographs and—crop them is the word, isn't it?—and I just wanted to ask if you would do this to my face; provided, of course, that it doesn't spoil the picture."

Murdock smiled, a little surprised at finding the man's reasoning as legitimate as his request. "What did this *Courier* fellow look like?"

"Well—quite good-looking. Light-brown hair, curly. Perhaps an inch or so taller than you and a little heavier; maybe a couple of years younger. He was bareheaded and wore a checked topcoat." The man allowed himself a small smile. "It seemed a little loud."

"What kind of a car?" Spencer asked.

"A Buick convertible."

"Stacy," said Spencer.

Murdock, still wondering about his visitor, added: "He's not in my department."

"Oh?"

"He's a reporter but he works some with a camera. Go upstairs to the City Room and ask for Ralph Stacy."

"Thank you very much." The man put on his hat and they watched him turn and leave the room.

"That's the second one this afternoon," Spencer said.

"What?"

"Looking for Stacy. The other was a dame."

"What kind of a dame?"

"Cute," said Spencer and clicked his tongue. "Small and dark and saucy. A little annoyed about something."

"Maybe it was you."

"Could be, but she wasn't here hardly long enough for that. She asked for Stacy and I said upstairs and she blew."

Murdock reached for his assignment spindle. "How's Bush's baby coming?"

"Hadn't come the last I heard," Spencer said, turning back to his novel. "Old Bush is still sweating it out at the hospital."

Murdock thought no more about the man who had witnessed the accident, and it is unlikely that he would have even seen Ralph Stacy for some days had it not been for Bush, who normally would have been on duty that evening. It was the top assignment that made the difference on this particular occasion; for while the bulk of the slips had to do with work for the following day, the top one read:

Citizens League Dinner at Parkview. 7:00 . . . Annual Award to Senator McCann.

Reaching for the telephone, he asked for the City Room. "What do you want on the McCann award?" he asked.

"Just the usual. Maybe a shot of the speakers' table and one of the Senator getting his award."

"Nothing on the dinner itself?"

"No. Stacy'll be covering that. If you'll have a man there by eight thirty or so it should be time enough."

Murdock hung up and told Spencer, who nodded. "I'll cover it," he said.

"No you won't," said Murdock, who did not want to be tied up all evening. "I'll cover it and you stay here and keep shop." He winked as Spencer groaned. "Eat early. It looks like a quiet night, so maybe you can finish your book."

The dinner at the Parkview was no different from hundreds of others Murdock had attended in past years. The waiters were starting to clear the tables when he arrived, and he stayed out in the hall smoking until it was time for the meeting to come to order and then went down front to get a shot of the toastmaster and the guests in the immediate vicinity.

There followed a boring interval that stretched on and on as the preliminary speeches were made, and as a result it was after nine thirty before Murdock got his shot of the presentation and the Senator. He ducked out as soon as he could and as he came across the back of the room to the doors he saw Ralph Stacy approaching from the opposite direction. They left the hall together, collected their coats. When they reached the sidewalk Stacy said he had his car.

"Down the block here," he said. "I'll give you a lift."

The year-old convertible shone like new and Stacy took an obvious pride in it as he swung it over to Commonwealth and started back toward town. At the Avenue he turned right and Murdock thought he would make another turn into Boylston; instead he kept on and then turned right again.

"I want to stop by my place a minute," he said. "You're in no hurry, are you?"

He turned again at a corner drugstore and then they were slowing down in a tree-lined, one-way street that was quiet and deserted, and bordered in this particular block by ancient brownstones for the most part, with here and there a more modern apartment house, all of them small. Most of the brownstones had been converted into flats and from his side Murdock could see a sign here and there in a basement window proclaiming small business endeavors or personal services.

Stacy was angling to the right toward a parking-space and now, as he cut in sharply and braked to a stop, a car started up behind them and on the opposite side of the street. Murdock was sitting with his equipment case at his feet and his still-open camera in his lap as Stacy cut the motor. Then, as the sound of the second car accelerated, it happened.

Stacy leaned over to reach for the key. He said: "Why not come up with me and get a quick one?" and Murdock was about to say he guessed not. Before he could speak the small window on the left side, rear, dissolved with an explosive crash and then, as the glass fell inside, he heard the two shots that sounded almost as one.

In that next instant Murdock had no time to be startled or afraid and what he did was little more than a reflex action born of experience and long training. He had a camera in his lap and instinct bade him use it. Without thinking he grabbed for the nearest handle and as the heavy door swung outward he half fell onto the curb.

But even in falling he was grabbing at the lens shield and giving a quick wind to the shutter. He had a flash-bulb in his coat pocket and as he jammed it into the synchronized unit he lifted the camera and pressed the shutter release.

The speeding car was fifty feet away as the bulb

splashed its light into the street and his first conscious thought was one of frustration when he realized that his attempt would almost certainly prove to be futile, not only because of the distance but because the car parked ahead partially blocked the one which had now disappeared. For another moment he stood there, a faint tremor moving up the backs of his legs as reaction hit him; then he slid back onto the front seat, not bothering to close the door.

Stacy, bent low with the key in his hand, began to straighten. Apparently he had been holding his breath, because as he leaned back he uttered the longest and loudest sigh Murdock had ever heard.

"Jesus!" he said.

Murdock glanced at him as his mind began to ponder the miracle of coincidence. The impending birth of Bush's baby had taken him out on an assignment that would normally not have been his; Stacy just happened to be covering the same event; Stacy wanted to stop at his apartment—

His thoughts hung there as he wondered if it was also coincidence that neither of them had been hit.

Pursuing the thought, he got out and went round the car. The segment of the left rear window was mostly gone, with only the metal-framed edges remaining. This suggested that the slugs had struck at an angle. The opposite window was intact but when he moved to that side he saw the two small holes about a foot apart in the canvas separating the side window from the one in the rear. He looked in at Stacy, who seemed not to have moved.

"Either we're lucky," he said, "or the guy was a lousy shot. Who would be gunning for you now?"

"What?"

Murdock's mind had gone back to remember another time when someone had taken a shot at Ralph Stacy.

That had been more than six months ago and was attributed to a series of well-documented articles that Stacy had done exposing the racket and corruption in the city's fruit and produce market and the union which dominated it. That time the end result had been the jailing of certain small fry, the cleaning out of the local by the president of the national union, the indictments, some of them still pending, of the top man himself.

"Last time it was the fruit and produce thing," Murdock said. "What is it this time?"

"Damned if I know."

"Then maybe you'd better think about it."

"Yeah." Stacy looked at Murdock. "Yeah," he said again and then, his composure regained, he said: "What about that drink now?"

"Let's get at it," said Murdock, and reached in for his equipment case. "I think I'll take this with me. I'm not so sure I want to ride back with you," he added with a grin, not knowing then that this would indeed be the case.

2

RALPH STACY led the way up the steep stone steps of the brownstone house diagonally across from his car. Both the outer door and the one leading from the entry-way to the vestibule were unlocked and the sound of music came faintly down the stairwell, swelling in volume as they mounted the ancient and thinly carpeted treads. There was but a single door at the second-floor landing and as Stacy reached for his key he jerked a thumb at the remaining flight of stairs.

"Great, hunh?" he said. "Every damned night, including Sunday."

"Radio?"

"Television. Seven to eleven. You can count on it."

He pushed open the door and snapped on a light, moving through a tiny entryway to a living-room that had a buffet at the far end and a partly open gate-leg table to indicate the dining-quarters. He had his Leica in his coat pocket and a small, limp-leather case in his hand, and he put these in the entryway closet before he asked Murdock what he'd have.

"I can give you bourbon or Scotch," he said. "Take off your coat. Sit down."

Murdock said: "Scotch," but by that time Stacy's attention had centered on a brown-paper package which lay on the small table next to the Governor Winthrop desk. From where he stood Murdock could see the label which said: *Anderson's—Haberdashery*, and now Stacy was tearing off the string and unwrapping the cardboard box. He tossed string, paper, and box into the wastebasket and held up three sport shirts for Murdock's inspection.

"Nice, hunh? Elinor must have been here, otherwise they'd be hanging on the doorknob." He glanced round. "I guess you know we finally separated. She got a furnished place around the corner on Leland Street last week. Moved out. We've been working up to it for a long time—and that reminds me." He reached for the telephone. "I want to give her a ring."

Murdock, still wondering about the incident on the street, had a little trouble following Stacy's swift digression. "What about calling the police?"

Stacy looked at him. "Did you get a good look at the car?"

"No."

"Is that picture you took going to be any good?"

"I doubt it."

"Then what's the good in calling the cops? No point in advertising this. Might give somebody else ideas. I don't want it to get to be a habit."

He glanced at a piece of paper which had been anchored by the base of the telephone, began to dial. Murdock eyed him curiously, aware that what Stacy said made sense, but finding it odd that the other should take the matter so casually. Apparently there was no answer at the other end of the wire and after listening another ten seconds Stacy hung up.

"Scotch, you said? Coming up."

He took his shirts into another room; then came back and disappeared through a swinging door to the left of the buffet. Murdock got a cigarette going and examined his surroundings, aware now that the furnishings, while comfortable enough, looked shoddy. The flowered slip cover on the sagging davenport was well worn along the binding, the carpet almost threadbare in spots. The upholstery in the three easy chairs was bunched and uneven, the lamps looked cheap, the combination radio and television console in the corner was an old one, so that only the desk, which seemed to be solid mahogany, had any character.

Stacy banged through the swinging door, a glass in each hand. Presenting one to Murdock with a bit of a flourish, he took a big swallow of his own and wiped his mustache—brown and a bit curly like his hair and worn rather long—with the back of his hand. He had nice teeth when he smiled, but his face was too soft-looking and puffy under the eyes to be called handsome, and that softness extended to his torso, clad now in a plaid suit that had a ready-made look about it. To Murdock, who was more clothes-conscious than some, the suit lacked distinction and now, his glance moving on to the checked topcoat Stacy had thrown over the back of a chair, he remembered the man who had come to the Studio that afternoon to ask about a picture. Before he could say anything the telephone rang and Stacy scooped it up with his free hand.

"Yeah," he said. "I only got in about five minutes ago. . . . What?" He listened, a frown grooving his brow. "So what?" he said. "No . . . why should I? . . . Okay, suppose he does?"

He listened some more, the frown growing. He tried to interrupt, tried again, finally made it. "Oh, all right," he said irritably. "Yes . . . okay . . . I said all right, didn't I?"

He hung up. He eyed his drink sullenly before taking another swallow. With that he shrugged and put the glass down.

"Look," he said. "I've got to duck out for a bit. I won't be gone more than ten minutes, so stay right where you are, will you? When you finish that one there's a bottle in the kitchen, so pour yourself another."

He had been backing toward the entryway as he spoke and then, not bothering with his topcoat, he opened the door and was gone.

Murdock sat right where he was, having no time to protest and not sure whether he should stay or not. He took some more of his drink and now he could hear, faintly, the sound of the television program from the floor above. A moment later, with no conscious effort on his part, he was thinking abut Stacy; not about the telephone call or the sudden departure but about the man himself.

It surprised him a little, now that he thought about it, how very little he knew about the man. He could not recall just when Stacy had come to the *Courier*, but he guessed it to be between three and four years ago. From Chicago—or was it Buffalo? He had never been close to Stacy, and he could not think of anyone on the paper

who was. If he had friends Murdock did not know of
them, but he had seen Stacy with a girl now and then
in some night spot or at the races, and he had heard
that for the past months Stacy had been attentive to that
blonde hatcheck girl—Murdock couldn't remember her
name—down at the Band Box.

He had met Mrs. Stacy at an office party soon after
they had come to town, had seen her twice here when
he stopped in for a few minutes on some office business,
but now all he could remember about her was that she
had seemed quiet and plain-looking, her manner contrasting sharply with her husband, who was loud in
manner as well as in dress. For there was a lot of the
back-slapper in Stacy and with it a brashness that no
doubt helped him in his work. He had an admitted
facility with words. He was an experienced man with
the Leica, and it seemed to Murdock that Stacy wanted
to be a big man and, perhaps because of some lack in
background or education, consistently missed his tar-
get. . . .

The sudden rasping of a buzzer stopped Murdock's
analysis and he looked at the door. When the sound was
repeated he put down his nearly empty glass and
stepped through the entryway. When he opened the
door a small, dark-haired girl in a green tweed coat stood
in the half-light of the landing.

"Hello," he said, smiling a little when he saw how attractive she was.

Without answering but watching him closely behind
her glasses, she started to move inside. Puzzled now but
still smiling, Murdock stood out of the way and then
closed the door while she stopped in the living-room and
glanced about. He saw then that she wore a shoulder
bag and had both hands thrust into the pockets of her
coat, and now, with the light better, he could see the

bright intentness of her hazel eyes and the tension working on her mouth.

"I've come for the picture," she said.

"What?"

"I'm Bob Hargrove's sister."

"Oh? Well—"

"I intend to get it if I have to find it myself," she cut
in, and with that she took her right hand out of her pocket
and pointed a gun at Murdock. "Where's your darkroom?
Is that where you keep your films?"

For the next second or so Murdock could only stare at
her. It was astonishment rather than shock that struck
him mute and left his dark gaze incredulous. The gun
was real enough, a foreign-looking automatic with wood
stocks that he thought might be a Mauser, but it simply
did not belong in this girl's hand. It was not just that
she was young and attractive; it was the very distinct
impression that everything about her, from her short
page-boy bob to her clear complexion and harlequin
glasses, suggested she had just come from Radcliffe or
Wellesley. As the thought came to him he wondered if
the intentness of her gaze was motivated by some de-
termination to show she was not afraid.

"All right," she said. "I'll look. . . . Down that way,"
she added, gesturing toward the inner hall. "You first, if
you please."

Murdock grinned at her again. He did not want to
make any mistake about the gun, because he knew that
in the hands of the inexperienced any involuntary pressure on the trigger might make it go off, but the curiosity
was working on him now and would not be denied. He
moved ahead of her, stopping at the first open doorway.

"Now what?"

"Turn on the light and then go to the other side of the
room."

Murdock did as ordered, finding himself in an untidy

bedroom with overflowing ash trays, a bureau top cluttered with masculine accessories, a clumsily made bed
on which were the three shirts Stacy had brought here.
A door in one wall, apparently leading to a closet, was
locked and after the girl had tugged at the knob she
backed from the room and told Murdock to come with
her.

The adjoining bedroom was neater because it looked
unused and the skirted vanity table was bare. The closet
door was slightly ajar and apparently the girl thought it
unimportant, since she merely glanced about the room
from the doorway.

At the end of the hall was a bathroom. After she had
examined this she came back along the other side. The
first door opened on the room she sought. Here, extending along one wall was a workbench on which were
trays, an enlarger, a timer, a ferrotyper. Underneath
were cabinets; on the left was a sink, and at the end of
the bench a small, double-deck filing-cabinet, its drawers approximately postcard size. One of these drawers
was partly open, the other lay up-ended on the floor.

"Where do you keep your films?" the girl asked.

She was standing quite close to Murdock now, the gun
hanging loosely, as though she had forgotten she had it.
He probably could have taken it away from her then, had
he wanted to bother with it, but the curiosity was still
working on him and instead he stepped to the cabinet
and pulled out the remaining drawer. Frowning when he
saw it was empty, he looked down at the one on the
floor, though he did not touch it.

"Probably here," he said, indicating the cabinet. "If
they were that size or smaller . . . If they were mine," he
added.

"What did you say?" she demanded, watching him
now as he started to back out of the doorway.

"Let's go into the other room," he said. "There's something you ought to know."

Some of the intentness had left her eyes by the time she reached the living-room, leaving them uncertain and wary. There was a film of moisture on her upper lip and the hand holding the gun trembled slightly and no longer menaced him. Still watching her as he reached slowly into the inner pocket of his jacket to get his billfold, he recalled what Spencer had said that afternoon about a girl who had asked for Stacy. Small and dark and saucy, Spencer had said. . . .

"Did you come to the *Courier* this afternoon?"

"Yes."

"Looking for Ralph Stacy? . . . Did you find him?"

"No, I didn't."

"You don't know him by sight?" He watched her shake her head, eyes wide open now as the color began to slip from her cheeks. "Then maybe you'd better put that gun away." He opened his billfold and smiled at her. "Save it for Mr. Stacy."

He put the opened billfold on the table next to his drink and moved back a step. The girl understood that she was supposed to look at the identification card in the glassine opening, but it took her five seconds to make herself do it. One glance was enough.

Her "Oh—" was a sucking sound and she stepped swiftly back. "Then you're not—"

"Stacy just stepped out," Murdock said. "He'll be back in a few minutes. . . . Why don't you wait?" he added as she began to back toward the entryway. "I could get you a drink and you can tell me what makes that film so important."

She was at the door before he finished, her cheeks like tallow and her poise gone. At that moment she looked like a very scared young lady and as Murdock stepped

toward her she opened the door and vanished without
bothering to close it behind her.

Just what motivated Murdock's next act he was never
quite sure. He did not stop to reason things out or even
to think. For he was more than curious now; he was con-
fused and perplexed, and he saw his camera standing
there beside the desk, and a second later he had it in
his hand and was reaching for a fresh flashbulb. Stopping
only long enough to reverse the film-holder and put the
latch on safe so he could get back in case the door swung
behind him, he started down. Below, he heard the click
of the vestibule door, and now he was swiftly descending,
still not thinking beyond the immediate problem.

The girl was reaching for the door of a waiting taxi
as Murdock came out on the high stone stoop. He heard
the driver kick the starter and as he lifted his camera he
called out to her.

"Oh, Miss—"

She half turned, her face directly toward him as the
flashbulb exploded to highlight her pallor. Then she
scrambled into the back seat and said something to the
driver. The cab got under way as the door slammed.
When it speeded up he noticed that it was a Blue & White
and that the last three numbers on its partly obscured
license plate were 111.

The upstairs door had remained open and he closed
it. He removed the film-holder and put it in the pocket
of his balmacaan along with the one he had exposed at
the dinner. When he had finished his drink he went over
to the window and stood looking out at the empty street,
the confusion still in his mind.

"Bob Hargrove's sister," he said, half aloud, aware that
the name was somewhat familiar but unable to place it.

Why, he asked himself, should a girl like that be running around with a gun? What sort of a picture was it that
she wanted, and why did she want it? There was no

answer to this and he knew there would be none until
he talked to Stacy, but the incident bothered him and
he waited motionless by the window, a straight-standing
man with a lean, flat-muscled body and an angular, bony
face that was at the moment somberly set. Somewhat
above average height but not conspicuously so, there was
a squareness to his shoulders that needed very little help
from his tailor, and his bathroom scales usually hovered
around one hundred seventy pounds when he came out
of his shower.

He stood unmoving as a car swung in toward the curb
below him but it took him a moment to focus on it, to
realize that it was small and foreign-looking. He thought
it might be a Hillman and now its door opened and a
bareheaded woman got out. He lost sight of her as she
crossed the sidewalk and he could not tell whether she
was coming into this building or not, and then his attention centered on another slow-moving coupé that
angled in on the other side of the street and parked ahead
of Stacy's convertible. He saw the lights go out, but whoever was driving did not get out and now Murdock
turned toward the desk, no longer interested and tired
of waiting for Stacy.

There were a blue leather desk set here, and two round
brass dispensers, one for a roll of stamps and the other
for Scotch tape, a pen in a black swiveled holder. He
took this out and reached for the small pad that was
there. He wrote: *Stacy*—intending to leave word that he
had gone back to the office, and then the buzzer sounded
again and he had to stop.

The woman who stood in the hall was the one he had
seen below. She wore a camel's-hair coat, the collar
turned up around a scarf. Her medium-length hair
looked wind-blown. She had an envelope in one gloved
hand and the other was thrust deep in the coat pocket.
Her voice, when she spoke, was low and faintly husky.

"Oh," she said when she saw Murdock. "I was—is Mr. Stacy in?"

Murdock stepped back. "Come in, won't you?"

She hesitated for a moment of quick inspection, her glance moving upward from shoes to face. She seemed to consider the well-cut gray flannel suit, the white shirt, and regimental-striped tie. When her gaze reached the top of the straight dark hair that was lightly touched with gray at the temples, she made up her mind.

"Thank you."

She stepped ahead of him, a tallish woman who moved with grace. She looked down at the envelope and Murdock could see that a name had been written across it in light-blue ink before she thrust it into her pocket. He asked her to sit down and she perched on the edge of the club chair, and, now that he had a good look at her, Murdock was impressed.

"Stacy'll be back any minute," he said. He glanced at his watch and saw that the ten minutes Stacy had specified had already elapsed. "Would you care for a drink?"

"No, thank you."

"Cigarette?"

She shook her head and, although she gave him a small smile this time, he was aware that some inner tension was working on her just as it had on Bob Hargrove's sister. The bulge of her hand in the coat pocket looked larger than it should and he wondered if she, too, was carrying a gun.

That he dismissed the idea as absurd was chiefly due to the fact that in his opinion this woman was a knockout. About thirty, he thought, give or take a year, with a well-boned face, a short, straight nose, and a full-lipped, seductive mouth. The light aureoling her head gave her brown hair an auburn sheen and her complexion, whether from nature or cosmetics, seemed flawless. It was the eyes, however, that impressed him most. Thick-

lashed and intriguingly green, they looked wise and intelligent and thoughtfully disturbed as they met his.

Aware that he had been staring, he reached for his
coat. "I was just going to write Ralph a note," he said.
"Maybe you'll tell him Murdock had to get back to the
office."

"You work with Mr. Stacy at the *Courier*?"

"Yes."

"And you're sure he'll be back?"

"That's what he said." Murdock indicated Stacy's glass.
"He left that, so I don't think he'll be long."

She nodded absently as he picked up his camera and
case. Her hand was still in the pocket of her two-hun-
dred-dollar coat but as he turned to go he saw her
settle back in the chair. . . .

When Murdock came out on the street he saw he was
right about the Hillman. It was a maroon convertible,
new-looking, and not too well parked. He glanced up
the street to see if Stacy was in sight and then, remembering the car that had parked soon after the Hillman, he
looked across the pavement. It was still there, a four-
year-old Ford, but there was no one in it now, so he
crossed diagonally and headed for the drugstore on the
corner in the hope of finding a cab.

He was about eighty feet from the lighted windows
when the man swung around the corner and came toward him. The two steps the man took before he passed
beyond the range of this illumination were enough to
tell Murdock that he had seen the face before. Beyond
that he could not think, and as they passed each other
he only knew that the other was as tall as he was, but
thinner, his face obscured under the pulled-down hat
brim.

In his years with the *Courier* Murdock had seen a
lot of faces he could not remember, and when the man
passed with no sign of recognition Murdock glanced over

his shoulder. Then, the disturbance of earlier incidents still working on him, he took another half-dozen steps, swerved abruptly, and stepped into the street between two parked cars. Glancing back along the street side, he waited. Ten seconds later the door of the Ford opened and the man climbed in. There was no sound of a motor, no sign of headlights. The street remained quiet and deserted, and after another half-minute of futile speculation Murdock continued to the corner, muttering to himself because he could understand no part of what had happened during the past half-hour.

He was lucky in getting a cab and when he came into the Studio fifteen minutes later he found Spencer nodding over his desk. He got out of his coat as Spencer came awake and now he gave him the film-holder he had exposed at the dinner.

"They'll want prints of those tonight," he said.

"How about the other one?" Spencer asked, eying the second holder.

"I'll handle it," Murdock said, and together they went into the corridor and turned into the black alleyway from which the developing cubicles opened.

For the first minutes they worked silently in adjoining cubbies; then Spencer said: "I almost forgot. Bush is passing the cigars tomorrow."

"Everything okay?"

"Yep. He phoned in an hour ago. A boy. Old Bush was so excited he could hardly talk."

Murdock said that was great and then he gave his attention to his work, knowing even in the dimness of the safe light that he had been right about the picture he had taken of the gunman's car. A further inspection in the printing-room a few minutes later confirmed the suspicion that the negative was worthless, and he left that one and the one of the girl to dry. Spencer was still working on his prints when, at eleven ten, the telephone rang.

The blunt, familiar voice of MacGrath, the managing editor, assailed Murdock's ear when he replied, surprising him somewhat since MacGrath was seldom around at that hour.

"We just got a flash from Heller at Headquarters," he said. "The word is that somebody killed Ralph Stacy in his apartment a few minutes ago. Shot six times. Heller's on his way there now but you stay put for a minute. I'm on my way down."

3

T. A. MacGRATH was a stocky, middle-aged man with a broad, muscular face, the mouth of which was usually warped by a cigar. The cigar, half-smoked and no longer burning, was anchored firmly in place as he swung into the anteroom, trailed by a blond youth named Wright, who had not been with the paper very long and now drifted to one side to look and listen while MacGrath sat on the edge of the desk.

"You covered that dinner with Stacy tonight," he said. "Where did you leave him? When did you see him last?"

Murdock sat motionless in his chair, shaken inside by what he had heard and unable yet to accept the news of Stacy's death. His first reaction, of shocked surprise, had given way to a jumble of thoughts and impressions which he had been unable to separate and now it took a tremendous mental effort to concentrate on what MacGrath was saying.

"He had his car," he said woodenly. "He was going to give me a lift and then he wanted to stop by his apartment." He continued, his dark gaze fixed inward as he relived the moment when the rear window of the convertible had dissolved under gunfire.

MacGrath leaned forward as he listened. He took the cigar from his mouth. "Why?" he demanded.

"I don't know."

"Well, what did Stacy say? You asked him, didn't you?"

"He said he didn't know who it was or why anyone should be taking a shot at him."

"I don't know what he was working on either," MacGrath said, "but maybe we can find out. The point is, nobody is going to shoot a newspaperman and get away with it. Not these days. Six shots sounds like a hoodlum job to me, and we're going to stay with this. We'll probably arrange for a reward and I'll want to talk to the other papers in case they want to co-operate, but I can tell you about that later."

He marched away, wheeled suddenly. "I found out Lieutenant Bacon's got the case and you've worked with him before, so let's do it again, hunh? Right now you may know more about it than the police and that should get us some co-operation. Don't worry about this job here"—he waved the cigar to indicate the whole department—"because we can take care of this routine for a day or two or until there's a break in the case. . . . What happened after you went up to the apartment?" he asked abruptly.

Murdock, in no mood for a cross-examination by MacGrath just then, omitted everything but the telephone call. "Stacy went out and said he'd be back in ten minutes. I got tired of waiting and left."

"But what—" MacGrath broke off suddenly, got himself in hand, tried again. "What the hell am I wasting time asking questions for?" he demanded of no one. "Here's what we do: Get your things and get started.

I'll phone Bacon at Stacy's place and tell him you were
there earlier. That should buy your way into the place
and get us a couple of pictures. Wright, here, is going
along to bring your film back. Stay with Bacon as long
as you can and when you finish come back here. I'll be
around. Okay?"

Murdock agreed. He spoke to Spencer, telling him to
put the films that were drying in his, Murdock's, desk,
and to send the other prints upstairs. He said he didn't
know when he'd be back.

The street of brownstones where Ralph Stacy lived
had a crowded look when Murdock and Wright got out
of the taxi and told it to wait. A half-dozen cars were
double-parked along one side, three of them police cars
and one an ambulance. A uniformed policeman stood in
the middle of the street to handle any traffic that came
along and on the sidewalk in front of the steps some
reporters were talking to another officer.

Heller, one of the *Courier's* Headquarters men, spotted
Murdock first. When he stepped forward to meet him
the other reporters grouped round him as the policeman
said: "Murdock? You're to go right up."

Ordinarily such an announcement might have brought
howls of objection and cries of favoritism from the other
newsmen, but they were silent now, understanding that
this was a different situation. One of their kind had been
murdered and they knew by now that Murdock had
been with the victim earlier and that the police needed
his help. The things he told Heller were what he had told
MacGrath, and they all listened silently, making a note
now and then since it was obvious that there could be
nothing exclusive about this part of the story.

"Hey, Murdock!"

The impatient policeman was moving up and Murdock

went to meet him. They started up the steps and then the officer noticed Wright.

"Who's he?" he demanded.

"He's with me."

"Uh-unh."

"He's going to take some film back to the office."

"Then he'll have to wait out here. The lieutenant said just you."

There was another uniformed man on the second-floor landing talking with two white-jacketed ambulance attendants, one of whom was leaning on a rolled-up stretcher like a farmer on his hoe. The officer nodded as Murdock turned into the open doorway, and then he was in the living-room, prepared now for the sight of Stacy's body on the floor but not finding it.

A laboratory man with a fingerprint kit was working on the telephone, a second detective was looking over the desk. The other two in the room stood off to one side talking in low tones. One of them seemed familiar to Murdock and now he jerked his thumb down the inner hallway. Just then an assistant medical examiner came out of the brilliantly lighted doorway of the first bedroom, his bag in hand. When he saw Murdock's camera and case, he nodded.

"You'd better hurry it up," he said.

The police photographer was starting to turn off his lights as Murdock stepped into the room and in that first second or two he was aware of nothing but the still figure stretched out on the floor and encircled by chalk marks. He could not see the face, which was turned toward the bed, but Stacy lay on his back, one arm outflung, legs straight and ankles crossed. His coat was open, his shirt, now almost entirely red-stained in the front, was unbuttoned and pulled up, apparently by the medical examiner.

Murdock swallowed hard and opened his equipment

case. He took out a fresh film-holder and two flashbulbs, his glance moving up now to see Lieutenant Bacon and Sergeant Keogh standing over by the window as the police photographer began to disassemble his equipment.

"Okay," Bacon said. "You're entitled to a couple for what you're going to tell me."

"I'll have to send the film down to the fellow I brought with me," Murdock said. "Your man wouldn't let him come up."

"That's okay too," Bacon said.

Murdock backed to the doorway, adjusted his focus, and took his first shot. He caught the ejected bulb as it popped out, inserted a fresh one, and reversed his holder. This time he pulled a straight-backed chair to the side of the room and mounted it for his second shot. As he stepped down and glanced about he saw that, with the exception of the body, only one thing had changed in the room since he had last seen it. The three new shirts still lay on the untidy bed, but the closet door which had been locked earlier now stood ajar and he could see the suits and slacks hanging inside, the traveling-bag and briefcase on the floor.

"You can wait out in the other room if you want," Bacon said. "I'll be with you in a couple of minutes."

The men with the stretcher were at the doorway when Murdock turned, so he went into the living-room and put his camera and case over against one wall out of the way. He took off his coat, folded it, and piled it on the case, put his hat on top. Telling the man in the hall that he'd be back, he took his film-holder downstairs and beckoned to Wright. Two photographers had joined the reporters, one from the *News* and one from the *Bulletin*, and Murdock called to tell them that the ambulance men would be coming down.

Upstairs, with the stretcher and its burden gone, he went over to the window sill beyond the desk and sat

down. The detective who had been looking over the
desk earlier had turned over the wastebasket and was
now on his knees examining its contents. Murdock realized then that the box and wrapping-paper were no
longer anywhere about and that there was nothing in
the basket but torn bits of paper and circulars and envelopes.

The pad on which he had started to write a message
to Stacy was still on the desk and now he touched the
detective's shoulder and pointed to the one word he had
written.

"When you get to that," he said, "don't let it bother
you. I wrote it."

4

LIEUTENANT BACON, the number-two man in the
city's Homicide Squad, was a tall, thin veteran with a lot
of thick, graying hair and a long, thin face that was for
the most part bleak and unsmiling. No one had ever
seen him in anything but a blue serge suit which was
always neat but apt to be shiny in spots; when the
weather was appropriate he wore a straight-hanging
dark-gray coat and, winter and summer, a gray felt hat
that he kept centered on his head except in moments of
exasperation or extreme provocation. Shrewd, experienced, and wise from long training without being bril-
liant, he had a dry, matter-of-fact way of talking and, so
far as anyone knew, no vices except perhaps a tendency
to overindulge at times in the use of his cigars, a little-
known brand called Little Wonder Panetelas, which
he bought by the box for five cents apiece.

There was a harried look in his gray eyes when he was

ready to question Murdock, and the lines around his mouth gave his face a tired expression, as though he understood the reverberations that would come with this murder of a reporter. There was a weariness in his voice too as he stopped in front of Murdock and said:

"All right. I understand you were with him tonight."

Murdock nodded gravely as he tried to erase from his mind the picture he had seen in the other room.

"You were also here for a while."

"Right."

"Does that mean you rode home with him?"

"He said he wanted to stop by," Murdock said. "He didn't say why."

"Okay." Bacon took a small breath, let it out slowly. What he said then indicated that his men had not been idle. "Now before we get to this business"—he glanced round at the room—"what happened to Stacy's car? It's parked across the road with the rear window on the left-hand side smashed out and two little holes in the canvas on the other side."

"Somebody took two shots at us."

"From where?"

"A car that had been parked farther down the block."

"What time?"

"As a guess, about ten o'clock."

"Suppose you give me the rest of it?"

Murdock did so, omitting only his futile attempt to get a picture of the fleeing car, since this seemed now to be pointless. He said he did not get a good look at the car, could not describe it, and, quoting Stacy, could give no reason why the attempt had been made.

A gleam of exasperation had begun to work at the corners of Bacon's eyes by the time Murdock had finished.

"It didn't bother Stacy at all, hunh? Wouldn't even call the police."

Again Murdock repeated what Stacy had said, and then, because the strain was still punishing him, he added: "Don't get tough with me, will you? I'll tell you what I can, but don't argue with me just yet."

He spoke quietly, bitterness cadencing his words, though none of it was directed at Bacon. The lieutenant understood instantly and was no longer exasperated. For another second or two he considered Murdock's brooding gaze; then he nodded.

"Okay for now," he said. "Either you were lucky—and you always are—or the guy was a lousy shot."

"I've thought about that."

"How far away was the car when it passed?"

"Maybe five feet when he passed, twice that when he opened up."

"So then you came up here with Stacy."

"To get a drink. He phoned his wife and she didn't answer," Murdock said and then explained what Stacy had told him about the recent separation.

"Ahh," said Bacon and looked interested. "You know where she moved to?"

"Stacy said around the corner on Leland Street. He looked at a number on a slip of paper under the telephone before he dialed."

"Who's got the slip that was under the phone?" Bacon asked and the man by the wastebasket said he had it. "Neilan!" The lieutenant waved at one of the detectives. "Let's get the address for this number. . . . Keogh," he added, "let's get some notes on this."

The sergeant, a blocky, blunt-nosed man with a hoarse-voiced and aggressive manner, moved up and took out a small notebook.

"Then what?" said Bacon.

"A couple of minutes later the phone rang," Murdock said, relating what had happened and what Stacy had said when he left.

Bacon pushed his hat back in a gesture of irritation, readjusted it.

"Jesus!" he muttered. "Stacy wasn't giving out much, was he? You don't know who called, or if it was a man or a woman, and you don't know where he went. But he left without a coat and said he'd be back in ten minutes. Only he wasn't. So what did you do?"

"Sat and finished off my drink," Murdock said, thinking now of the girl and the gun and the silly routine that he had gone through with her.

Without trying to analyze his motives he simply could not picture that girl coming back to kill like that, even in panic. She had been scared when she left, she knew he had taken her picture. He knew her last name, could probably check the cab with the number ending in 111, and, from the driver's route card, find out where he had taken her. Until he knew more, why involve someone like that who was, in all likelihood, quite innocent of murder? Aware that he could conveniently remember her later if necessary, he conveniently forgot to tell Bacon about her now.

"I got tired of waiting," he said. "I went over to the desk and started to write him a note and then this woman came."

The lieutenant said: "Hah!" this time. "Now," he said, "we're getting somewhere. What kind of a woman? What did she want? She rang the buzzer and you opened the door, is that right?"

"She asked for Stacy. I told her to come in, and when I said he'd be right back she did."

"Describe her."

Murdock did.

"Now classify her."

"How?"

"You get around. You know how. What would you

say she was? Rich, poor, a bum, a hooker? What's your
opinion?"

"She was a knockout," Murdock said. "Well groomed,
well cared for. She had gloves on, so I don't know
whether she was married or not, but if she was a hustler
she moved at a high level. If you want a guess I'd say she
was about thirty, probably either married to or kept by
some guy with money enough to buy her two-hundred-
dollar camel's-hair coats or anything else she wanted
within reason."

Bacon glanced round to see if Keogh was keeping busy.
Satisfied about this, he said, talking to himself now:

"She rings the buzzer. You let her in. She wants Stacy
and agrees to wait and you leave her sitting here. Now,
have you got any idea—any idea at all—of what she
wanted?"

"No," said Murdock. "But she had an envelope in her
hand when she came in. From where I stood—this is before she put it back in her pocket—I noticed something
was written on the front in light-blue ink. It could have
been a name."

"Lieutenant." The detective who had been checking
the desk and wastebasket offered an envelope, empty
now, that had been torn open at one end and crumpled.
"What about this? It was in the wastebasket."

Bacon passed it to Murdock. When he saw that Stacy's
name had been written across the front of it he nodded
and said that could be it.

"Also," he said, "I think she may have been followed
here."

He told Bacon why he thought so and what he had
seen from the front window.

"What kind of a car?" Bacon asked.

"A Hillman."

"You didn't get the number, hunh? . . . And you think

the car that followed her and parked across the street was a forty-nine Ford coupé. Color?"

"Dark. Blue or black or dark green." He explained how he had seen the man pass the lighted windows of the drugstore, how he had watched until the man climbed into the Ford.

"But you don't know who he was?" Bacon pressed.

"I've seen his face before, but I don't remember where and I didn't get a good look at him when we passed. He was about my height but a little thinner, I'd say. Wore a snapbrim brown hat and a dark topcoat."

Bacon looked thoughtfully over the top of Murdock's head and rocked up on his toes. When he eased back he reached for one of his panetelas, took out a small penknife, and began to manicure one end. When he had the cigar drawing to his satisfaction he again gave Murdock his attention.

"So," he said, "the last thing you're sure of when you started looking for a cab—by the way, what time was that?"

"Somewhere around ten thirty."

"Then the way you left it, the dame was still in the apartment and this guy in the Ford was waiting outside and Stacy hadn't come back."

Murdock nodded. "When did you get word?"

"The telegraph bureau got it at eleven three."

"Got what? A call?"

"And one we couldn't trace. A man's voice said there'd been a shooting on the second floor of this address, and hung up.

Murdock kept thinking about the woman in the camel's-hair coat and wondering what had been in the envelope. Now he said: "What did Stacy have in his pockets?"

"I'll show you."

Bacon took a cloth bag from Keogh and up-ended it

on the desk. Pushing the cigarettes and the three folders
of matches aside along with two handkerchiefs, he enu-
merated the remaining articles.

"The four dollar bills were in his left-hand trousers
pocket, the change and those keys in his right. The billfold in an inside pocket, along with the bankbook." He
indicated the key chain. "One key to the car, another to
the apartment. We don't know about the other two."

"One might fit the bedroom closet," Murdock said and
knew it was a mistake even before he'd finished the remark. For how could he say that he knew the closet was
locked when the girl had tried the knob earlier? Why,
without some prior knowledge, would he think of the
closet at all? The exact same thought apparently occurred to Bacon. He cocked his head an inch to the left,
his gaze suddenly curious.

"What makes you think so?"

Murdock shrugged and did the best he could, his
glance evasive. "I don't think so. It was just a thought."

Still watching him, Bacon handed the keys to the detective named Neilan and ordered him from the room
with a jerk of his head.

"How much was in the billfold?" Murdock asked.

"Sixty bucks. Plus registration, driver's license, press
card—nothing that helps us any. Neither does the bankbook—yet. A checking-account, so we won't know until
tomorrow what his balance is. One thing, though—" He
took out his cigar to make sure it was burning evenly,
smoothed the wet end down, replaced it gently.

"He had some fairly good-sized deposits for a newspaper guy," he continued, glancing through the book.
"Some five hundreds, a couple of eights. They don't pay
you monthly down there at the *Courier*, do they?"

Murdock said no, and then, as though prodded by
some inexplicable thought process that had been waiting
for a chance to be heard, his mind digressed and he re-

called the man who had come to the *Courier* that afternoon to ask about a picture Stacy had taken. He spoke
of this now, repeating the conversation as best he could;
then, at Bacon's insistence, he described the man.

"Do you know what happened to that picture?"

"It could still be on the Leica roll," Murdock said.
"Stacy brought the camera up here with him. It's in the
closet."

"We found it, Lieutenant," someone said.

"Let's have it. . . . Jorgenson," he said to the Headquarters photographer who was sitting on the arm of the
chair. "See if there's a film in that camera."

Neilan came back with the chain of keys to announce
that one of them fitted the closet lock. Bacon gave Murdock another quick look, but when he found Murdock
intent on other things he made no comment.

"There's a film, all right," Jorgenson said. "If this
counter is right he's taken about six exposures."

"Wind it up," Bacon said. "When you get it developed
we'll see if Murdock can pick out this guy."

"There's another thing, Lieutenant." Jorgenson began
to rewind the film as he spoke. "There's a pretty well-
equipped darkroom down the hall. I went over it."

"So?"

"Well, it's a funny thing, but I didn't find any films in
it and I understand there weren't any in the desk here,
or in the bedroom."

"I don't get it," Bacon said, frowning.

"Well, a fellow that takes pictures generally has a file
of his exposed negatives, at least the good ones he likes.
There's a two-drawer card-size file in there that might be
okay for a thing like that, but it's empty and one of the
drawers was on the floor."

"Oh." Bacon chewed on that one, glanced at Murdock.
"You got a file like that at your place?"

"Sure, for the negatives I want to keep."

"At home? . . . Maybe Stacy kept his at the office," he said when Murdock nodded.

"He could have," Murdock said, "but he didn't use the Studio equipment much. It's not set up for miniature work. You can do it, but—"

"Okay." Bacon walked away, turned, and came back, head down now and cigar smoke trailing. "You get the Stacy woman's address?" he said to Neilan. "Then let's go see her."

He began to tell his men what he wanted them to do and Murdock, paying no attention, went over to put on his hat and coat. When he picked up his camera and case Bacon came up to him.

"Do you know her?"

"Slightly."

"Then maybe you'd better come along. It might be a little easier to have someone from the *Courier* help break the news, and if you knew her—"

He let the sentence dangle, but the thought remained with Murdock as he followed Bacon and Keogh down the stairs and climbed into one of the police cars.

5

THE APARTMENT Elinor Stacy had moved to was not quite two blocks away, a five-story structure in a street of similar, smaller buildings, most of them forty years old or more, all of them tired-looking and discouraged. The brick façades were weathered and stained, much of the trim needed painting, and most of them were walk-ups.

Perhaps because of the extra story this particular building had an automatic elevator, and the new-looking card over the vestibule mailboxes announced that Mrs. Stacy occupied apartment 5-C. A police car with two plain-clothesmen had followed Bacon over, and everyone rode up to the top floor, where Bacon told Keogh and the detectives to wait in the hall until he called them.

"Maybe you should speak to her if she asks who's there," he said to Murdock as he put his thumb on the buzzer button. "If she knows you're from the paper—"

"Sure, sure," Murdock said shortly. "Old Murdock can take it. He'll break the news."

"Don't get sore," Bacon said without animosity. "It's got to be done and you can help." He gave the button another push and presently, leaning close to the panel, he said: "Here she comes."

"Yes?" a voice from inside said. "Who is it, please?"

"Kent Murdock, Mrs. Stacy. From the *Courier*."

There was a moment of silence and then the key rasped in the lock and the door opened to reveal a woman clad in a quilted robe and low-heeled mules, her brown hair caught at the nape with a ribbon.

"Yes, Mr. Murdock," she said, hesitating then as her glance moved on to Bacon.

Bacon nudged Murdock, who said: "This is Lieutenant Bacon, Mrs. Stacy. Could—we come in a minute?"

"I'm sorry." The woman stepped back, a faint smile starting in her shadowed face. "Of course."

They moved past her to a room that was dimly lighted by a floor lamp. When Elinor Stacy had closed the door she pressed another switch to light a ceiling globe, thereby revealing a squarish room which bore so obvi-ously the stamp of mediocrity that it only could have been rented "furnished." A studio couch stood against the wall between the two windows; there were a spindly-legged table covered with magazines and a tiny, plas-tic-cased radio, a Boston rocker, an easy chair, two tufted-cotton rugs, a painted table desk, two floor lamps with imitation parchment shades.

Murdock saw all this at a glance and then, as he turned back to the woman, he noticed the discolored and slightly swollen spot beside her left cheekbone. Other than that her face seemed pale and slack, shiny in the absence of any make-up.

"It's about Ralph," Murdock said awkwardly.

"Sit down, please, Mrs. Stacy," Bacon said.

She backed toward the couch and eased down on it, knees together and her gaze fixed on Bacon.

"I'm afraid it's bad news," he said and cleared his throat. "Somebody shot him tonight in his apartment."

"Shot him?" The words came out hollowly, the shock not yet showing. "But how could that be. I—I was over there and—"

"Oh?" said Bacon as she paused. "When was that?"

"Earlier. I went over to—" She stopped again before she whispered: "He's dead, isn't he?"

Bacon nodded. He cleared his throat again, and as he related the circumstances Murdock's thoughts remained with the woman and the three other times he had seen her. Coming over in the police car he could not remember what she looked like, the impression he had from that office party nothing more than the name and the vague mental picture of a plain-looking woman with little style who wanted earnestly to be liked. It was the same way on the two occasions he had stopped to see Stacy at home. She was simply there in the background, a wife, a woman, pleasant enough and making no attempt to intrude but leaving no lasting impression.

Even now as he watched her react to Bacon's grim news he did not know why. She was not homely. There was nothing wrong with her features, taken individually. The face was longish, her brows needed attention, her hair was a neutral brown. The eyes were intelligent and

well spaced, but other than that it was a face that had
neither animation nor distinction, reflecting little in the
way of character, personality, or even age. He had the
feeling somehow, though he did not know why, that here
was a woman who had never been young, and had he
noticed her on the street he might have put her down as
a spinster, perhaps someone's secretary, and probably a
good one.

Now, with Bacon's explanation finished, she simply sat
there staring wide-eyed at him, her lips parted, the bruise
contrasting vividly with her flat-white skin. An awkward
stiffness had taken possession of her body, and her hands
had clenched as they rested on her knees. She wet her
lips and swallowed.

"I—I can't believe it," she whispered finally.

"It's a rough deal," Bacon said. "I only wish I could
give you time to get used to the shock, but I'm afraid
I can't, Mrs. Stacy, under the circumstances. There are
some questions I'll have to ask you—there will be more
later—but in a case like this time is often extremely important."

"I understand, Lieutenant."

"Would you like a glass of water? Or is there anything to drink here that we could get you?"

"There's nothing to drink. I'm quite all right. I think
I'd rather talk."

Bacon pulled the chair away from the table desk and
sat down, balancing his hat on his knees. Murdock eased
into the one easy chair and listened while Bacon spoke
of the two men in the car who had shot the glass out of
Stacy's convertible. He asked if she had any idea what
might be behind this attempt and when she shook her
head he said:

"There was another time, six or eight months back,
when the same thing happened, wasn't there?"

"Yes, there was."

"And do you know why?"

"Ralph said it was because of that series of articles he wrote."

"About Joe Calenda and his rackets," Bacon said and glanced at Murdock. "I read them. Calenda is appealing one conviction now and he's under indictment on four counts of perjury, not to mention income-tax trouble yet to come. Your husband was responsible for much of that investigation and I wondered if you knew of any new threats he might have received."

"Not recently."

Bacon shifted his weight on the chair. He hesitated as he studied the woman and when he continued his voice was quiet and, for Bacon, solicitous.

"I'm going to be frank with you, Mrs. Stacy."

"I wish you would."

"What I have to say is not to be taken as any insinuation that you killed your husband, but as a police officer I am forced to consider that possibility."

"I understand that too."

"The man, or men, that shot at your husband and Mr. Murdock earlier may have come back later to do the job. It's quite possible. If so, it's hoodlums we'll be looking for. On the other hand it may be something quite different, and when a married man, or a woman, has been found shot, the wife, or husband, is naturally under some suspicion, especially when there has been a separation, as I understand is the case with you."

"Yes."

"Was the separation because of another woman?"

"Yes—that is—"

She paused and Murdock, watching her closely, could tell by now that her eyes were light blue and showed no trace of tears. If there was any grief here it was well hidden by the expressionless mask that had taken possession of her face. Her voice, when she spoke, was soft but colorless and showed no hesitation.

"There had been other women," she said, "but never seriously or for long. There is a woman now. A blonde girl who works at a place called the Band Box—"

"Her name?"

"Nancy Larkin. At least that's what she calls herself. However," she said before Bacon could interrupt, "she's not entirely to blame for our separation. She brought it to a head, hurried it a little perhaps, but the real reason is a combination of things that had been building over the years. I'll try to explain it if you like."

She waited for Bacon's approval and said: "Ralph and I came from the same small town outside of Chicago. We were in high school together and are the same age— thirty-two. He got a job on a Chicago newspaper and later I did too—as a clerk in the classified department. We were married there and we both worked and we put off having children. Later we went to Buffalo and Ralph was making more then, so I stopped work, but somehow we never seemed to have anything."

"He handled the money?"

"Yes. Then after we came here things seemed to change. Maybe it was my fault for staying home and being a housewife. I've never been too extravagant with clothes and I didn't want to be spending money in beauty parlors, which may have been a mistake for a woman who is naturally plain-looking. Because, you see, Ralph's work took him places I couldn't go. He was out practically every evening while I stayed home. He always had the excuse that it was his work that took him to these night clubs and parties and the dog track. I knew he wasn't always alone, but I wouldn't have minded so much if I'd gone along some of those times."

She glanced down at her hands and said: "Maybe I wouldn't have minded at all by that time—you know, of course, that we had separate rooms—if there'd been money enough so that I could have had some new clothes and perhaps a little car so I could get out and make some friends of my own. I finally got a job in an office, part time, nine to one. I'm still working. And then this girl came along and I simply decided it wasn't worth it. It seemed to be a one-way, dead-end street and I wanted to get off before I got too old, so I told him I was moving out."

She hesitated, her eyes starting to fill as she continued:

"Maybe that's why I can't seem to feel the sort of grief just now that a normal wife should feel. I suppose that sounds callous to you, Lieutenant, but I'm not much good with pretense. It would not be convincing and I'm sure you would know it. Tomorrow, perhaps, when I have to go through Ralph's things, when I remember other times, it will be different; I'm sure it will be different. But now"—one hand moved to her breast—"there doesn't seem to be anything there. I still don't believe it even though I realize that such things happen—to other people. You must understand that the man I'm talking about is the man of the past two or three years; not the man I married."

Bacon nodded. He said he thought he understood.

Then, her digression having reached its conclusion, Elinor Stacy took a breath and lifted her chin, her unspilled tears drying. "Last week," she said, "I went to see a lawyer."

"Could I have his name, please?"

She gave it, waiting while Bacon wrote down the name and address before she continued.

"And he said he'd talk to Ralph so there could be some sort of property settlement and a reasonable alimony payment. Ralph said he'd go to the lawyer, but he didn't, and that's why I went over there tonight."

"Yes," said Bacon. "But before we get into that could you tell me if Mr. Stacy had any insurance?"

"Yes, he did. A policy for ten thousand dollars."

"You're the beneficiary? . . . Now, do you know how much he had in the bank?"

"No. He'd never tell me."

"Savings accounts?"

"If he had one I didn't know of it."

"All right." Bacon's hat was getting in his way, so he put it on the floor and leaned forward. "You went over to see your husband tonight. What time was that?"

"I think it was somewhere around nine thirty when I got there."

"Did you expect him about then?"

"No. But I had my key and I intended to wait. There was a package for Ralph hanging on the doorknob and I brought it in and put it on the table. I took off my coat—"

"I notice you have a bruise on one cheek," Bacon said. "An accident or did someone strike you?"

"Someone hit me."

"Who?"

"I don't know."

"What?"

"It was a man, but I'd never seen him before and—"

"Pardon me," Bacon cut in, a trace of irritation beginning to manifest itself. "Suppose you start at the beginning and take your time and tell it in your own words, Mrs. Stacy."

"I had just turned on the television set," she said, "when the buzzer sounded. When I opened the door these two men pushed right in."

"Two men?" Bacon scowled at her, forgetting he was going to let her tell her story. "What did they look like?"

"One seemed rather young, with blond hair and dark glasses and no hat. The other was heavier and older. He wore a blue coat and a gray hat and he had a—well, a sort of flat, muscular face and thick brows."

"Go on."

"I asked them what they wanted and they said my husband and I said he wasn't home. 'We'll have a look around, then,' the older man said. 'Where's his dark-room?' Well, by that time I was angry and a little scared. I told them they had no business there and to get out or I'd call the police."

She hesitated, pale lips tightening and distance growing in her eyes. "I started toward the telephone and the younger man grabbed my arm and swung me about and I started to scream and that's all I remember. I don't know whether I was knocked out or fainted, but when I came to I was on the floor and the television was still on. I didn't dare get up for a minute or two—until I was sure they had gone—and then I—"

"Did you look in the darkroom, Mrs. Stacy?"

"Yes, I did."

"Did you notice anything different about it?"

The question brought an instant's hesitation before she said: "I don't know very much about the darkroom, Lieu-tenant. It looked all right, except—"

"Except what?"

"Well, there was a drawer on the floor—it was empty —and another drawer like it was partly pulled out on the counter and that was empty too."

"Did your husband keep films in that cabinet?"

"I think he did."

Bacon glanced over at Murdock, his frown suggesting that he did not care much for what he had just heard. He considered the woman a silent moment.

"You didn't stay there, Mrs. Stacy?"

"No, I didn't. I was furious at myself and the two men, and my head ached and I felt sick all over. I didn't want to see or talk to anyone just then, so I turned off the television and put on my coat and came back here."

"What time would that be—as a guess?"

"Before ten. I'm not just sure."

"Did you happen to see anyone?"

"Not that I remember."

"It would simplify things if we could have some corroboration." Bacon hesitated and then, very casually, he set his trap.

Murdock was waiting for it because he had known the lieutenant a long time and had watched him work. The two men that Elinor Stacy had mentioned had upset Bacon's calculations because in his book the old-fashioned murder motives were best. When there was a triangle situation, as there was here, he understood that the soundest of motives were usually such things as jealousy, hate, or some sudden vindictiveness. Beneath his calm and courteous treatment of this woman there remained the suspicion that the answer might be here. He had been thinking all the time and weighing his values and now he was ready to test the theory.

"A phone call would help," he said in a voice that seemed to be throwing the thought away, "if there were any?"

"There was one."

"Oh?"

Murdock sat very still and now he could feel the tension working on him. Unconsciously he held his breath as he studied the woman, who seemed hardly to have moved since she had sat down. At the moment her pale face revealed nothing at all. Only the eyes spoke of her intelligence and they were at ease.

"It rang soon after I got here," she said.

Bacon's glance flicked to Murdock to check with him, to be sure such a time was consistent with the call that Ralph Stacy had tried to make.

"And who was it?" he asked.

"I don't know." She paused, an apology in the faint
smile that touched her mouth. "I didn't answer it," she
said. "I had taken off my dress and I was in the bathroom
bathing my face and the water was running. I didn't
hear it until after I turned off the faucet and I wasn't
sure I wanted to answer it anyway, but I did start to,
and then it stopped."

Bacon's sigh was audible, his expression defeated.
"That's too bad," he said lamely. "It would have helped."
He picked up his hat. "I appreciate your co-operation,"
he said. "And I'm afraid I'll have to ask for a little more
of it."

"Naturally I want to do what I can," she said in that
same colorless voice.

"If you'll get dressed now I'd like you to ride down to
the precinct station and make a statement. I'll provide
the transportation for you and it shouldn't take long.
You won't have to go into this background you have
given me; just the things you did tonight, the facts as you
recall them. Also"—he felt for the gold chain draped
across his vest and pulled out a watch—"I'd like your
permission to search this apartment."

"Now?"

"Yes. I can get a warrant if you insist and that may
take some time at this hour. Someone will have to wait
with you until I get it—"

She interrupted him with some wordless sound. She
took hold of the lapels of her robe and drew them close.

"You still think I may have killed him, is that it,
Lieutenant?"

"Let's put it another way, Mrs. Stacy. Right now I
don't know who killed your husband and until I do it's
my job to consider those who were closest to him first.
The sooner I know you didn't kill him, the easier it will
be for you and the sooner I'll be able to give my attention to other possibilities."

Murdock watched her stand up, finding no sign of resentment in her face. Outwardly there was no indication that any of this had touched her and her voice remained controlled as she said Bacon was quite welcome to search the apartment.

"I'll get dressed," she said, and then she clop-clopped across the room, her back straight and her shoulders high.

Bacon grunted softly when the door closed behind her. He walked in a small circle, reached for a cigar, and then replaced it. He glanced up at Murdock, head still bent and his gray eyes speculative.

"What do you think?" he asked.

"I think you're wasting your time," Murdock said. "There's no jealousy in her any more. You'll need another motive."

"She's no glamour queen," Bacon said. "But she's got a pretty good mind." He glanced about the poorly furnished room. "It isn't much, is it?"

Elinor Stacy was back in less than five minutes, wearing a beige woolen dress and carrying a cloth coat and a bag. The ribbon was gone from her hair and she had drawn it back to a bun that seemed somehow to accent her plainness.

"May I see your handbag?" Bacon asked.

For just a moment then a gleam of resentment flickered in her light-blue eyes. Bacon saw it. He said:

"Your husband was shot six times, Mrs. Stacy, but we haven't found the gun."

She said: "Oh—" and gave him the bag. When he had glanced inside he thanked her and returned it. Then he went over to the door and summoned his helpers.

"This is Sergeant Keogh," he said. "Mrs. Stacy. When he has finished here the sergeant will drive you to the precinct station while you make your statement and then bring you back."

"Then—I'm not to go with you, Lieutenant?"

"I'd rather you were present while the search is being made. That way there'll be no misunderstanding later. . . . By the way, do you have Nancy Larkin's address?"

She gave it to him and he said: "That's about a block from your other apartment, isn't it?"

"Yes."

He thanked her and put on his hat. He reached for the doorknob and then turned back.

"One more thing, Mrs. Stacy." He paused to make sure he had her attention. "You didn't telephone your husband tonight, did you?"

"No, I didn't."

"And he didn't come here?"

"No. I haven't seen him at all. I told you that."

Bacon opened the door and nodded to one of the detectives. "Come on," he said. "You can drive."

6

THE APARTMENT house where Nancy Larkin lived looked withered and shabby, presenting at this hour, with the front windows darkened, an air of desertion. Most of the tile was gone from the unlighted entryway and Bacon and Murdock had to pick their way past two strollers and a collapsed baby carriage. Food smells hung thickly in the dimly lighted foyer and the thin rubber treads echoed hollowly as they climbed to the second floor and went along the hall to the last door on the right.

"This," said Bacon as he knocked, "I'll handle myself."

It only took one knock. Nancy Larkin opened the door almost immediately. She was dressed in her Band Box costume—a tight black skirt and a white blouse cut round in the neckline so that it did not quite cover her shoulders—and even from where Murdock stood at Bacon's shoulder he could smell the liquor on her breath.

"Yes?" she said.

"Miss Larkin?" Bacon moved in, causing her to drop back. "Lieutenant Bacon. We'd like to talk to you a few minutes."

"About what?"

"Police business."

He was inside then and he let Murdock close the door as he watched the girl back up until her calves touched a studio couch which had been covered with chintz and supported three pillows and an overdressed doll. She sat down, her gaze fixed.

"All right," she breathed. "Is something wrong?"

Bacon sat down and motioned Murdock to do likewise and now he was a different Bacon. With Mrs. Stacy he had been dealing with a woman who had just lost her husband with tragic unexpectedness and, at least in the beginning, he had treated her with the sympathy demanded by the occasion. Nancy Larkin belonged to another category in Bacon's mind. She was to get exactly the amount of consideration he thought she deserved, and he began his interrogation with simple directness.

"You're a friend of Ralph Stacy?" It was a statement rather than a question.

"Y-yes, I am."

"Did you see him tonight?"

"No."

"When did you see him last?"

"Why—I—it was last night."

"You work at the Band Box as a hatcheck girl."

"Yes."

"What time do they close down there?"

"The bar closes at one—"

"I know that; that's the law."

"—but it's later than that before—"

"Why aren't you working now, then?" Bacon said, interrupting her again.

"I did. I mean I was there earlier. I had a headache and—" She broke off, lips trembling as her voice rose. "Why are you asking me these questions? I have a right to know." She stopped again, her eyes wide. "Something's happened to Ralph. That's it, isn't it?"

"Stacy's dead," Bacon said.

"Oh, no! No—please."

"Somebody shot him. A couple of hours ago. In his apartment."

For another instant the girl looked at him, her young face stiff. Then, as though some invisible force had released an emotional drawstring, it fell apart and she buried it in her hands.

Murdock's face was suddenly hot and his collar felt tight. He gave Bacon a look of mild disgust and Bacon shrugged silently and leaned back to reach for a cigar. For the next minute or so he gave it his attention and there was no sound but the rasping sounds that came from deep inside the girl. Her ash-blond hair had fallen forward to cover most of her hands and she was bent almost double, her elbows jammed between her thighs, the points of her shoulders exposed as the sobs shook her.

Murdock did not have to look at her to remember what she was like. Because he liked the trio at the Band Box, he had seen her there often, a tallish girl with an erect way of carrying herself that did nice things for her willowy, neatly rounded slenderness. Her hair was worn in a long bob to show it off to its best advantage, her mouth was wide and mobile and quick to smile. Her voice was small and she had at times a sort of wide-eyed helpless look, either real or assimilated, that made the customers more willing to let go of a half-dollar or a bill instead of the usual quarter tip. . . .

"Miss Larkin."

Bacon had his cigar drawing and was ready to continue. The girl looked up, tears glistening on her cheeks, and now her face was white and stiff, her hands clenched, her mouth tight and stubborn-looking.

"I think you'd better get your hat and coat," Bacon said.

"You mean—you're going to arrest me?"

"That depends on you." Bacon paused, his gray gaze probing and intent. "You can tell the truth about tonight now and we can ride down and get a statement. That way you can come back and sleep in your own bed. . . . Or," he said with added harshness, "you can keep on lying and sleep in a cell which the city will provide."

"But I—"

"Just a minute." He waited for her attention. "Somebody telephoned Stacy between five and ten minutes after ten tonight. Mr. Murdock was there and heard it. . . . According to Mr. Murdock," he said, stretching the truth now, "the call was from a woman. Stacy left immediately. He said he'd be back in ten minutes. He didn't take his coat, so he wasn't coming very far. We've already talked to Mrs. Stacy. She didn't make that call, so that leaves you."

"All right."

Nancy Larkin swallowed and her eyes began to fill again. Suddenly she began to shake all over and now Murdock understood why she had been drinking. She had been expecting Bacon, or someone like him, and she'd needed courage and there was no other way for her because she was so young.

"Yes, I called him," she said in her small voice.

"Why?"

"Because I was afraid."

"Of what?"

"Of what Jack Frost might do. He was drunk and he said he was going to look Ralph up and—"

"Who's Jack Frost?"

"He has the trio at the Band Box. His name isn't really Jack. It's Edward. But he thought people would remember Jack Frost better, so he—"

"All right," said Bacon when the chatter got too much for him. "You phoned Stacy. He came over and you told him Frost was looking for him."

"Was *going* to look for him," she corrected. "At intermission. That would be about ten thirty when the singer comes on. She has her own accompanist."

Bacon looked at Murdock. "From the Band Box to Stacy's is maybe ten minutes? . . . So what did Stacy say?" he continued as Murdock nodded.

"He laughed at me. He said he could handle Jack and that I was to stop worrying, and anyway Kent Murdock was at his place—Ralph's—in case he needed any help."

"Frost was jealous, is that it? You'd given him the air for Stacy and—"

"I loved Ralph," she whispered.

Bacon considered this. He considered the ash on his cigar and looked round for a place to dump it.

"You knew the Stacys had separated," he said. "On account of you?"

"Not—just that. Ralph said his wife wanted to divorce him and it was about time. He said it should have happened long ago and if she didn't he'd leave and take me with him." She hesitated and then began to shake again, as though some new thought was rekindling her fears. "But Jack wouldn't do a thing like that. He—he's not that kind."

"You still like him, hunh?"

"Of course I like him. I've always liked him. He helped

me get my job. He was kind and thoughtful and—" The words trailed off and she tried again, her voice barely audible and eyes fixed on something far beyond the borders of the room.

"He had a blackjack tonight," she said. "He might have tried to beat Ralph up, but he'd never shoot him down like that, never."

"All right, Nancy." Bacon rose. "Get your coat."

"But—you said I wouldn't be arrested if I—"

"Nobody's arresting you," Bacon said, his tone more kindly now. "I just want to get the facts down on paper. We'll check your statement and if we find out you've been lying to us—"

He let the implication ride as the girl stood up and readjusted the top of her sagging blouse. She shook back her blond hair and pulled her stomach in. When she had composed her tear-streaked face she began her high-heeled walk toward the open doorway of the adjoining bedroom.

"If I were you," Bacon said, "I'd leave that bottle alone."

"I will," she said without looking back.

Bacon turned slowly in his inspection of the room. He glanced under the three pillows on the couch, examined the doll. There was a low chest topped by an imitation Chippendale mirror at one wall and he went over to examine the drawers. When he had finished here he picked up the handbag on the telephone table and checked its contents.

"I want to get back to the office," Murdock said.

"Sure," said Bacon. "We'll find a cab for you."

He buttoned his straight-hanging coat, resettled his hat, working on his cigar in small puffs until Nancy Larkin came back wearing a black coat and fresh make-up.

When Murdock got back to the *Courier* building at twelve forty the trucks were backed up to the loading-platforms and the presses were rumbling in the basement. Up in the Studio T. A. MacGrath sat tipped back in Murdock's chair, his heels on the desk, an empty coffee carton beside a crumpled ball of waxed paper. For once the trade-mark of his cigar was missing.

"Sit down, Kent," he said. "Bring me up to date."

Murdock put his camera and case away and took off his hat. He left his coat on as he pulled up a chair, and there was no interruption as he related briefly the things that had happened. When he finished MacGrath took a legal-size envelope out of his pocket and handed it over.

"This was delivered to Stacy tonight," he said. "We don't know who put it on his desk, but when we found out what had happened they brought it to me. It didn't come through the mail, so I opened it."

Murdock, disturbed by something in the managing editor's tone, studied him a moment before he looked at the envelope. He saw then that across its face and crudely printed in pencil were the words: *Ralph Stacy—Courier Building.* Down in one corner it said: *Personal.*

Murdock took out the folded sheet, and as he opened it a thin stack of hundred-dollar bills slid into his hand. He counted ten of them and put them on the desk, an odd emptiness beginning to work on his stomach. He swallowed against it, finding it impossible then to control his thoughts and imagination. It took a conscious effort to unfold the paper because he was afraid of what might be inside.

The message, in the same crude printing, read: *This is a token payment for your nuisance value. Tonight was only a warning. Stay out of the North Shore or we zero in.*

Murdock put the bills inside the paper, replaced both in the envelope, which shook in his fingers as he returned it to MacGrath. For the moment he could think of nothing to say, so he waited, his dark gaze troubled, his mouth bleak.

"It looks," said MacGrath quietly, "as if the guy in the car who took those shots at you missed on purpose."

"It figures," Murdock said, "but it doesn't mean Stacy was trying to put the bite on anybody."

"It also figures," said MacGrath, "that this crowd didn't come back later and knock him off. If they had they never would have bothered leaving the money or the message." He rubbed his blunt jaw and the day-old beard gave off a scraping sound. "Had you heard he was working on anything on the North Shore?"

"No."

"It was no assignment for us. It could have been another of his ideas for a series of his own, like the one he did on Joe Calenda and his rackets." MacGrath put clasped hands behind his neck and gazed ceilingward, his tone both speculative and reminiscent.

"There was a city editor once," he said. "In the East, but not here. He's not a city editor any more. He's not even in the newspaper business. He had what seemed like a cute deal for a shakedown because he never had to work on anything himself. His reporters would do it on assignment. He'd pick out some beach resort town—say in Jersey—and assign a couple of his men to make a preliminary investigation of vice and gambling conditions, always making sure that the word got out. By asking the right questions in the right spots his reporters practically guaranteed that the word would get around. Then all he had to do was sit back and wait. Usually it didn't take long before he'd get a good score. If the price was right the reporters were called off and that was the end of the investigation."

"Stacy was no city editor," Murdock said.

MacGrath seemed not to hear. "He wasn't very well liked, was he?"

"I never heard he was disliked."

"I've been doing some talking tonight. Nobody around here seemed to be what you'd call a friend of his. He was a loner, a close man with a buck. A good man too, especially on features. He knew how and where to dig for his facts and he'd keep at it until he had what he needed." MacGrath's gaze came down and his feet swung to the floor.

"I'm worried," he said. "I've held up on this reward thing. We can't play this big and raise a stink and then have it slap us in the face. This thing"—he shook the envelope and then thrust it into his pocket—"could be nothing more than a warning that Stacy never expected or knew anything about. The point is, somebody killed him and we want to know who. If he died because he was working on something for us we're going to build a reward and give it all the space it needs. If it's something else, a personal motive not connected with his job, why, that's different, but still we have to know."

He leaned forward, his gaze intent. "We've got plenty of brains on this paper, Kent. More per man than the police department will ever have, even though we don't have the equipment. Remember that. I can name you a dozen men who not only can come up with facts as well as the police department but know more people. Use them."

Murdock stood up with MacGrath. "What you mean is you'd like to get the answer before the police do."

"In this case, yes. It would help."

Murdock shook his head, dark eyes sardonic. "A little luck might be more useful than brains."

"You've always had your share." MacGrath gave him a fleeting grin. "So stick with it, son. Percolate. Do favors. Play with Bacon. Snoop. At least for another twenty-four hours this is the top assignment in the plant. By that time my hunch is that, even if we can't break the case, we'll know what we should do at this end."

7

IT WAS ten minutes after one when Kent Murdock arrived at the Band Box, and although the street door was already locked from the outside people were still coming out, so it was a simple matter to get in. In the half-light of the foyer he saw that the little brunette who usually sold cigarettes was working in the coatroom, and in the doorway beyond, a cluster of women stood waiting while their escorts made payments on their hats and coats.

The main room was nearly empty now, the bandstand dark. In the alcove on the left the only light was the one over the cash register and here the bartender was checking receipts. Murdock went over and perched on an upholstered stool.

"Hello, Harry," he said.

Harry was a big man with a bald head and heavy jowls. He had been a bartender for a great many years, working here and there but mostly in night clubs. When one folded he always seemed to find a job in another and during the summer he took his family to the shore and worked in a club bar or another night spot.

"Hello, Mr. Murdock," he said. "You're just too late tonight." He waved to indicate the empty back bar and the locked cupboard beneath it. "Closed tight."

"I don't want a drink, Harry." Murdock lit a cigarette and pocketed the matches that had been stuck in the black ash tray. He pushed his hat back and blew smoke at Harry's back. "Just a couple of minutes of conversation," he said. "Can you talk and count at the same time?"

"I can try."

"Jack Frost gone?"

"With an escort. Two precinct dicks, I think. At least I recognized one of them."

"When was that?"

"Oh, maybe a half-hour ago."

"Did you hear about Ralph Stacy?"

Harry stopped counting. He made a notation on the register strip. He turned to put his big hands on the bar and leaned on them.

"Yeah," he said gravely. "The boss told me just after they took Jack away."

"They didn't question you?"

"No, but they will," Harry said wearily. "About eight o'clock tomorrow morning just when I'm sleeping good they'll be pounding on the door."

Murdock grinned at him. "Let's rehearse what you're going to tell them, Harry. In the morning your wife calls you and the cops are waiting in the living-room when you go in in your bathrobe, and then they say: 'Did Jack Frost leave the club at intermission time last night?'"

"And I say: 'Yes.'"

"Was he drunk?"

"Yes."

"Did he have some trouble with Nancy Larkin?"

"I don't know about trouble, but they were arguing pretty loud. I don't know much about it; I was busy at the bar."

"Did Nancy leave after that?"

"I didn't see her go, but I understand Beryl—you know, the cigarette chick—took over the checkroom." Harry reached both hands under the counter and brought forth two strong-looking highballs. "I haven't had a drink on the job for years," he said, "but I like a nightcap before I go home. Cheers."

Murdock gave him a crooked smile as he ground out his cigarette.

"Thanks, Harry," he said, "but I don't need it."

"Neither do I," said Harry. "It's bourbon, if you can go for that. But if you hear the outside door open, drink fast."

Murdock reached for the glass and they drank together, silently and with dispatch. Harry dumped ice into the sink and put the glasses on the drainboard.

"Jack came back about eleven," he said and leaned close. "And this I don't tell the cops. I never saw a guy sober up faster in my life. He was reeling a little the last I saw of him and when he comes back he could walk a chalk line."

"He wasn't often drunk, was he, Harry?"

"Practically never."

"He was still carrying the torch for Nancy Larkin."

"You could be right. I wouldn't want to say."

"And Ralph Stacy cut himself in."

"Let's say he was here most every night and almost always took her home afterwards." He leaned forward again, his voice curiously soft for a big man. "She was a nice kid, Mr. Murdock. If Jack Frost went overboard for her you could hardly blame him."

He looked off over Murdock's head and said: "She's only twenty-one. I understand she wanted to be a singer and worked here and there with small bands, mostly for peanuts, and in between did a turn as a waitress, or a hostess, or a hatcheck girl, like here. Now I've seen a lot of these kids, Mr. Murdock, and kicking around, working in and out of traps like this, they get tough inside— maybe they have to be for self-protection—and they've got their eye on the fast buck. They develop hard little faces and tough little minds and when you get them out

in the daylight they don't look so good. Most of them
are lazy, a lot of them are stupid, and some of them have
about as much morals as a rabbit."

He leaned back, as though realizing that he had made
more of a speech than he had intended. He grunted
softly; then he grinned.

"End of speech, Mr. Murdock. End of rehearsal. I've
got to put my cash away."

Murdock stood up. "Nancy wasn't like that, hunh?"

"No, she wasn't. She could put a fresh John in his place
when she had to, but she wasn't hard inside. She still
wanted to sing; at least she'd been working with Frost
up until a couple of weeks ago. Like I say, she was a nice
kid. . . . Well, good night, Mr. Murdock."

Murdock said good night. When Harry's back turned
he slid a dollar bill on the counter and moved unnoticed
from the alcove.

On his way home Kent Murdock stopped in an all-
night lunchroom for a sandwich and a glass of milk, so
that it was somewhere around two thirty when he
climbed the stairs of this building where he lived. His
apartment was on the second floor and he had his hat
in one hand, his key in the other as he approached the
door. He let himself in quietly, as was his custom, not
bothering to snap on the wall switch for the entryway
light. There was another switch round the corner of the
living-room wall. He reached out in the darkness, found
it; then, unaccountably, he stopped, his arm outstretched
and his breath held.

At that instant his reaction was an instinctive one and
motivated by his sense of smell. For there was no sound,
no movement in the inky blackness that engulfed him.
On the way home he had been doing what he could to
discipline his thoughts and erase from his mind the
things that had happened that night. He did not want

to lie awake thinking about them and he concentrated
on the promise of a soft bed as a reward for his labors
and his weariness. Now, in an instant's time, his imagination was racing and as he stiffened there he had the
intuitive but certain knowledge that someone was in the
living-room.

It was an odor which set up the sudden chain reaction,
an unfamiliar and as yet indefinable smell, and he did
not stop to analyze it. Knowing only that it did not belong here, he listened, and now there came to him the
faint but unmistakable rhythm of someone's breathing.

It lay ahead of him, growing more distinct as he concentrated on it. He let his own breath out through his
open mouth and inhaled once more. Again he listened.
Then, deciding that the sound he had heard came from
the direction of the davenport, he slid silently along the
wall to a floor lamp which he knew was there.

He put his hat back on so both hands would be free.
He located the lamp presently and slid his fingers over
the bowl-like metal surface of the shade. This was
mounted on a swivel that acted like a universal joint and
he turned it so that the cone of light would focus away
from him. When he was ready he pressed the switch and
the light beam jumped across the room, its brilliance
spraying the davenport like water from a hose.

Poised there, his weight on the balls of his feet so that
he could move in any direction, he stood right where he
was. Something on the davenport which should not have
been there told him instinct had been right, but it took
him a few seconds to understand what it was.

Slowly then he let his hand swing down, a grin eras-
ing the fatigue on his lean face as the tension slid away
from him and he understood the nature of the menace
he had prepared for. He saw the green tweed coat on
the chair. Its owner lay curled on the davenport, her

face obscured but her dark hair spilling out on one of
the cushions.

He knew before he saw her face that this was the girl
who had come to Stacy's with the gun, and he did not
speculate as to why she was here or how she had got in,
but walked over and stared at her a silent second or two
before he reached down and gently shook one huddled
shoulder.

In the moment of her waking she looked about twelve
years old. She stretched like a kitten with her eyes still
closed, some sleepy sound coming from her lips that
seemed related to a purr. Reluctantly she opened her
eyes. She looked up at him as from a great distance; then
the eyes went wide and clear, one hand flying to her
cheek as she bounced to a sitting position and braced
herself on one arm.

"Oh!" she said, her young face flushed with sleep and
confusion. "I didn't hear you come in."

Murdock watched her straighten her harlequin glasses
and then, playing it straight and trying not to grin, he
said:

"Haven't I seen you before somewhere? . . . Miss
Hargrove, isn't it?"

She was as quick as she was cute. She came in on cue.

"That's right," she said. "Betty."

"How do you do?"

Murdock put out his hand and she took it.

She said: "How do you do, Mr. Murdock," and then,
to give her a chance to get her feet on the floor and
straighten her skirt, he went over to turn on the room
light and put out the floor lamp.

"How did you get in?" he asked as he slipped out of
his coat and removed his hat.

"I woke the superintendent or janitor or whatever he
is down on the ground floor. He didn't like it." She
brushed her hair back and gave him a shy smile. "I told

him I was your niece and I'd just come in from New York. You'll probably hear about it in the morning."

Murdock grinned back at her, no longer quite so tired. He swung a chair round and straddled it, arms folded on its back. For another moment he studied her, intrigued more by her spirit and independence than by the fresh prettiness of her small face.

"Why?" he asked.

"I had to talk to you and you weren't here, so—" She fumbled for a word and it wasn't there, so she glanced down and picked at the hem of her skirt. "I heard about Mr. Stacy on the midnight news broadcast."

Murdock waited, giving her no help. Presently, her face still averted, she said: "I knew you'd taken my picture, and you knew my name. I thought you might even be able to trace me by the taxi if you wanted to."

"You thought I'd go to the police."

"Didn't you?"

"Not yet."

She let her breath out in a small sigh. "Thank you," she said gratefully.

"I looked your name up in the phone book," Murdock said. "I found an address for a Robert Hargrove."

"That's my brother. We're sharing an apartment until he gets married."

"He's the golfer, isn't he?"

She nodded and Murdock, recalling the name now, knew that he had seen Hargrove's picture in the sport pages as one of the district's leading amateurs. He seemed also to remember that Hargrove worked for one of the downtown brokerage firms.

"Was your father in the Navy?"

"A retired captain," she said. "He's in Washington now. I stayed here with Bob. I—I'm trying to write."

"You acted pretty tough tonight," he said. "What were

you going to do to Stacy if he gave you an argument, shoot him?"

"Of course not."

"What, then?"

"Scare him."

"Suppose he didn't scare?"

"Why, then"—she glanced up at him and made a face—"I probably would have got mad and run home."

"But what made you think he would scare?"

"Because," she said flatly, "I think anyone who would blackmail a person is a coward."

Murdock looked at her in astonishment. "Wait a minute!" he said sharply.

She blinked at his tone, but her eyes never wavered and now, as the shock of her words came through to him, a nerve tightened somewhere inside him and his throat went dry. Then, as a quick but meaningless anger came on the heels of his reaction, he fought to put it down because he knew that was not the way.

Deliberately then he took time out to get a cigarette, to offer her one, and provide a light. He put his forearms back on the chair.

"Tell me about it," he said.

She eyed him anxiously a moment and he could see her swallow. "It happened last summer," she said, her eyes now focused on her cigarette. "Bob had been in some tournament and afterward he got a little drunk and some of them went to this cheap club down around Hingham. Before the night was over he was too drunk to know what he was doing and he came out of the entrance with these two blonde entertainers, or hostesses, or whatever they were, hanging on his neck. I don't know what Mr. Stacy was doing there and neither does Bob. He doesn't remember any picture. He says he doesn't even remember the girls and"—she looked up as though challenging Murdock to refute her—"I believe him."

"So?"

"Bob forgot all about it, what little he remembered. Then last October he got engaged to Janet Lowry."

"Is that the Chestnut Hill family?"

"Yes. They're to be married in May and that was when the photograph of Bob came in the mail—last October, I mean. There was a telephone number on the back of it and Bob called it." She reached forward to put out her cigarette, looked up suddenly.

"You must remember I didn't know anything about this until just the other day, but the picture scared Bob and he had spent most of his money on the engagement ring and so he could only pay a hundred and fifty dollars for the negative. Then, the day before yesterday, he got another photograph, and I saw that one and made him tell me what happened. At first he wouldn't. He said he'd take care of Mr. Stacy in his own way and I was afraid he would, so I kept after him until I got the truth. I made him promise not to do anything until I'd had a chance to see what I could do."

The sickness had been growing in Murdock with each word. So intent and discouraging were his thoughts that his cigarette singed his finger before he remembered to put it out.

"Was there any note that time?"

"Just one on the back of the photo. It said that for two hundred dollars Bob could have the negative. That's the first time Bob knew that there were two pictures."

"There probably weren't," Murdock said, knowing how the job had been done.

"But now that Mr. Stacy is dead, suppose someone finds that negative?"

"If anyone should, it could never be used. Neither could Stacy have used it without being tossed in jail."

"But he could send a print to Janet Lowry," she argued. "And wouldn't that be nice?"

She had other things to say, but Murdock did not hear them. He knew that what this girl said must be true and yet he argued with himself, protesting silently that this could be an isolated case and as such proved nothing. For like other honest men who were brought up in the newspaper business and liked their work, he understood that the free press was one of democracy's most powerful institutions.

It was nothing that he had ever put into words, but the belief was ingrained, and he knew that along with the rights and privileges of this free press there was a moral responsibility not to abuse such privileges. Very few newspapermen did and those who weakened were never newspapermen for long. The newspapers themselves were their own watchdogs for the most part, but now and then something happened which, in the minds of shallow thinkers, discredited the whole profession.

Right now he was convinced that this girl was telling the truth as she knew it, and he could not forget the two men who had knocked Mrs. Stacy down and, from all appearances, cleaned out Stacy's file of negatives. Taken together, these two incidents gave credence to a suspicion that Murdock had hitherto refused to admit. Now some hastily contrived apparatus in the back of his brain remained closed, like a sticky shutter, sealing off for the time being the obvious answer as being not yet worthy of acceptance.

He cared nothing about Bob Hargrove's escapades, his engagement, or his coming marriage to this girl from a prominent family; he cared very little more in a personal way about what had happened to Stacy. What concerned him was the integrity and good name of the profession he followed and so, like that, he demanded more concrete proof before accepting a conclusion that might prove to be superficial.

"Don't worry about any more pictures," he said as he

came to his feet. "And if anyone should ever ask me I'll tell them you've got more spunk than good sense."

"I deserve that," she said gravely, "even though it isn't very flattering." She rose and shook out her skirt. "And about tonight? Will you have to tell the police?"

Murdock had put the chair in place and now he saw the tweed coat. On impulse he stepped over and picked it up. The weight of it told him the gun was still in the pocket, and when he took it out and pulled back the slide he saw that the chamber had been effectively plugged, rendering it harmless. When he pulled out the clip and found it empty he remembered the postwar drive which had been instigated to neutralize war souvenirs so that they might be kept without penalty. Pleased by what he saw, even though he had never really considered her as a suspect, he said:

"The answer is no."

"No?"

"No police. . . . Is this your brother's? . . . Did you know it wasn't loaded?"

"I don't know anything about guns," she said, "except how you hold one. I've seen enough movies for that."

He went over to the telephone and ordered a taxi for her and less than three minutes later a horn tooted out front. He held her coat for her. He said two-way radios were a wonderful thing when you needed a cab.

"Scoot," he said. "It's late."

He walked her to the door and she hesitated here as he opened it. She looked up at him, her smile shy again, a softness in her hazel eyes that was both admiring and grateful. What he saw pleased him secretly and embarrassed him too. He felt she was about to thank him and he did not want to be thanked, so he turned her to face the hall, gave her a gentle shove and a small spank.

"Be a good girl now," he said, and closed the door before she could reply.

8

KENT MURDOCK was at his desk the following morning shortly after nine in spite of MacGrath's suggestion that he stay away from the office for a day or two. It was a habit he could not easily break and he was still occupied with handing out assignments when the telephone rang.

"Mr. Murdock," the voice said. "This is Elinor Stacy."

"Yes, Mrs. Stacy."

"I was wondering if you could stop by this morning. There's something I'd like to discuss with you if you're not too busy. I'd like your advice if you could possibly—"

"Certainly," Murdock said. "Where are you? At your place?"

"At Ralph's."

"Fifteen minutes?"

"That would be fine," she said. "It won't take long."

Murdock finished the job at hand, took one of Bush's cigars, and congratulated him on the birth of his son. He put on his hat and coat and told Taylor, his assistant, that he would check with him later. Hailing a taxi outside the building, he rode to Stacy's apartment, noticing as he paid the driver that the convertible was still parked across the street.

His first impression when Elinor Stacy opened the door was that she looked much better than she had the previous night. Except for a touch of lipstick her face lacked color, but the simple black dress she wore gave a trimness to her figure that had been absent before and her brown hair, still worn in a bun at the back, had a softer look. Her intelligent light-blue eyes met his glance squarely and she shook hands as she admitted him.

He could see then that she had already begun the task of putting the apartment in order. Stacks of letters, receipted bills, papers of one kind or another had been piled on the floor near the desk. The small, sectional bookcase had also been emptied, the hard-cover and paper-backed volumes neatly piled in front of it. There were, she said, three things she wanted to discuss.

"First is the car," she said. "I suppose it should be sent to some garage, but I don't know which one."

"Do you want to sell it?"

"I don't really know yet. The main thing now is to get it off the street. You see, I've never learned to drive and—"

"Why not take it to the Buick place?" Murdock said. "They can keep it until you decide what you want to do. I'd be glad to drive it over for you, or I'm sure they'll come and get it if you'll call them."

She said that would probably be best. She did not want to inconvenience Murdock and she would telephone the garage later.

"The second thing," she said, leading the way down the hall, "is the matter of Ralph's clothes."

She stepped into the bedroom and Murdock saw that the closet was empty, the contents of this and the bureau drawers covering the bed. He counted three suits, two odd jackets, some extra slacks, a raincoat, and an overcoat. There was a pile of shirts, another of underwear, pajamas, socks, neckties, handkerchiefs.

"Would it be your idea to sell them?"

She shook her head, frowning now as she chewed on her lower lip. "I don't think so," she said. "I understand secondhand-clothes people pay very little and I think I'd rather they went to someone who would appreciate and use them."

Murdock said he did not know of anyone personally but that there were organizations that would be delighted to have them. He would be glad to make inquiries at the paper and get a list of such agencies, and she could then telephone some of them and make up her mind. She said she would appreciate having such a list.

"The thing I really need your advice on," she said when they went back to the living-room, "the real reason I called you, is this."

She sat down in the desk chair and motioned him to another. She reached over and took an envelope from the window sill. She glanced down at it and then looked out the window though there was nothing there to see but the budding branches of an oak tree.

Murdock waited, making no attempt to speculate on what the envelope might contain, but taking the opportunity to study her. Her feet, clad in black suède pumps, were flat on the floor and it surprised him a little—though he did not know why—to find her ankles neat and well turned, the calves shapely. She would, he knew, never be considered pretty, but with the right kind of advice from some stylist, the proper clothes, and a different hairdo, she could be attractive enough. What happened then would depend on her personality rather than good looks. . . .

"I'm sorry," he said, aware that she was watching him.

"I found this when I cleaned out the bookcase. It was sealed and I opened it. When I glanced inside and saw what was there I decided I should call you."

Murdock took the envelope and his sense of touch told him what was inside even before he lifted the flap.

"Films?" he said. "Negatives?"

"Yes."

The simple thought that Stacy had hidden some negatives would, under normal circumstances, have meant little to Murdock. In the light of what he knew plus the suspicion that he had shut off in the back of his mind, this new discovery jarred him badly. He could feel his fingers start to tremble as the apprehension built up inside him, and suddenly he was afraid to make any inventory of the envelope's contents in front of this woman. He could not meet her gaze, nor could he ignore her, and so, because it was necessary to do something, he took a quick look inside. What he found were several strips of film of four frames each, a lot of odd, single films, and some small envelopes. He did not know what these might contain and at the moment he did not care. His one thought right then was to accept the situation casually and to pretend as best he could that the discovery was of no great importance.

"You don't know why he kept them?"

"I have no idea. I saw that they were films and I thought first of the police and then I thought of you because you worked with Ralph and you're a photographer. I don't know yet whether they belonged to him or the paper, but you'll be able to tell about that, won't you?"

Murdock said he thought so. He said he was glad she had called him. "I doubt if this is anything for the police, but I'll take them along if it's all right with you."

He hesitated, his face set and trouble working in the disturbed darkness of his eyes. He pocketed the envelope, glad indeed that she had thought to call him, and then, because it was something he had to know, he forgot pretense and said:

"I'm not suggesting this, Mrs. Stacy, but it's important for me to know if, in your knowledge, Ralph ever collected money for any of his pictures."

She looked right at him, nothing changing in her face. "You mean blackmail, don't you?"

"Well—not necessarily," said Murdock, flustered by her

directness and hating the word. "I thought you might
know—"

She cut him off with her low, unemotional voice. "I'll
be as truthful as I can," she said. "No, I did not know.
Ralph hadn't discussed his work with me in some time.
The thought never entered my head until this morning
when I found that envelope. I didn't go through it because those things would mean nothing to me. But I
thought they might to you. I thought you'd be able to
tell, and then you'd know what to do—if anything. That's
why I phoned you."

Murdock had heard enough and now he stood up and
reached for his hat. He said he appreciated what she
had done and that he would be in touch with her later in
the day. She said she expected to be there until late afternoon and he said he would call her. After that he got
out fast.

Lieutenant Bacon was at his desk reading a report
when Murdock walked into the little office opening from
the detectives' room. He had one of his half-smoked
panetelas in his mouth and his grunt of greeting was
good-natured, so Murdock sat down in the only vacant
chair and stretched his legs, a small smile on his mouth
that belied the somber darkness of his eyes.

"What have you got for me?" Bacon said when he put
down the report.

"Nothing."

"Then what do you want?"

"Information."

Bacon's thin face warped into one of its rare grins and
he reached back on the desk and picked up a 11 x 14
print. "Maybe we can make a deal," he said. "You first
. . . Remember the guy you told me about that came to
the paper yesterday afternoon looking for Stacy? Said

there'd been an accident and didn't want his picture in the paper?"

He waited for Murdock's nod and said: "Well, that film was still in Stacy's Leica and here's a blow-up of that shot. Pick out the guy for me."

Murdock examined the print which showed a car with a bent fender and a broken windshield. There were a dozen or more spectators in the background and the face he sought was in the middle, a bareheaded man in a white coat. He pointed and Bacon circled the man with his pen; then examined the picture more closely.

"The story you gave me was that this guy was afraid his wife would see the picture because he was with some other woman. I don't see any woman close to him."

"Neither do I," said Murdock.

Bacon pondered the matter, scowled, and then yelled out through the open door. When a detective appeared he gave him the photograph.

"Find this character," he said. "Lower Washington. Accident happened yesterday afternoon, so you can find out exactly where. The guy with the white coat. Probably works right around there."

"Maybe in a laundry," the detective said, "or a counterman in a restaurant or cafeteria."

"You'll find out when you see what kind of stores and shops there are in that neighborhood," Bacon said and waved him away. "Tell him it's a routine questioning and bring him down." He watched the detective leave and then turned back to Murdock. "So what do you want to know?"

"Whether you still like the love-triangle motive."

"Certainly I like it. I'm going to keep on liking it until somebody proves me wrong."

"It's a quartet," Murdock said.

"With Stacy dead, it's a trio. The wife, the other woman, and her ex-boy friend. The wife feels abused.

She's given the best years of her life to Stacy and now
he's taking up with a cute blonde and the wife won't
stand still for it."

"If Elinor Stacy was jealous she's quite an actress."

"So maybe she's an actress."

"She was home when Stacy called."

"She could have gone back," Bacon said, but there
was little enthusiasm in his argument. He put his cigar
aside and picked up a sheet of paper. "I have to give
her this, though. Her story of the two men who gave
her the lump on her cheek checks. One of my beagles
located a neighbor of hers. Lives down the street on the
other side, and around ten or fifteen minutes of ten last
night he was walking the dog and he saw these two
hoods come out of Stacy's building and get into a car.
One he remembers was bareheaded and blond."

"Figure Nancy Larkin," Murdock said.

"I will," said Bacon. "She gave Frost the brush for
Stacy. She probably figured Stacy would marry her if
he could get a divorce, but now that Mrs. Stacy moved
out and was going to get a divorce, maybe Stacy changed
his mind. She phoned him last night, but what she
said happened after that is only her story and doesn't
have to be true. Stacy could have been getting ready to
blow town, for all we know. He could have told the
Larkin girl off and come back to his place, and she could
have run after him with a gun and gone boom-boom."

He ran out of breath and leaned back. "I can't prove
any of that yet, but it's early. Same with Frost. We know
when he left the Band Box and when he came back. He
was gone about a half-hour, which would be time
enough."

"Are you holding him?" Murdock asked.

"No. He was down here until nearly four this morning
and we got a statement out of him. He admits shooting
off his mouth at the club when he was drunk. He

admits he had a blackjack, but he insists he knows nothing about a gun. According to him, he started to Stacy's but couldn't find a cab, so he stopped in a place for a drink—we're checking that—and then when he came out he turned chicken. He says he walked around until he sobered up a little and then went back to work. If I can punch a hole or two in that story I'll haul him in and book him."

Murdock had been listening to everything Bacon said, but his mind was not entirely attentive. He knew that a case could be built against all three people, but Bacon would need more supporting evidence than he had. Now, as his mind went on, he thought of something else.

"How about Stacy's bank account?"

"I've got a man over at the bank now." Bacon picked up his cigar, brushed the ashes off with a match, and carefully lit the butt. "I also checked on that part-time job the wife has and I don't think there's anything at that end. The guy she works for gives her good marks; says she's pleasant, co-operative, that Stacy never came in the office. . . . But before you go," he said, "give me a guess on this: Why did those two hoods want the films Stacy had in his darkroom—if that's what was in that little filing-cabinet."

Murdock said he did not know and Bacon eyed him aslant. "I've heard," he said thoughtfully, "that Stacy had been poking around the North Shore. I'm looking for some tie-in with that shooting-up of Stacy's car. The guy that took those shots couldn't have been more than five or ten feet from you when he opened up."

"He wasn't," Murdock said.

"And who's crazy enough to hire a gunman to knock a guy off if he can't shoot any better than that?" He bunched his lips around the cigar butt. "Looks more like a warning to me. Stacy was working on something and he was getting too close and this was a way of telling him to lay off or else." He paused to take another look at Murdock. "Who'd know about that over at your place, your man MacGrath?"

Murdock stood up. Remembering the note and the hundred-dollar bills MacGrath had shown him the night before, he said MacGrath would probably know if anyone did.

"If MacGrath happened to hear that rumor," Bacon muttered, "and I heard the rumor, you can bet the North Shore boys heard it too. . . . Keep in touch with me, hunh?" he said as he turned back to his reports.

9

KENT MURDOCK had steadfastly refused even to touch the envelope Elinor Stacy had given him until he had reached the privacy of his apartment. He had come here directly from Police Headquarters and now, with his hat and coat out of the way and his pipe going, he sat down in his living-room, taking the wing chair by the window where the light was best. Dumping the envelope upside down on the rug, he picked up the first small envelope that came to hand. As he reached inside he knew that it contained a negative and a contact print, and the first glimpse of that print left him startled and incredulous.

All he knew in that first moment was that it was a nude. In a picture that small it was difficult to tell much more, and he paid no attention to the face but put it aside and went to his knees beside the pile of negatives and small envelopes. He had but one thought in mind now as he went quickly through the negatives and prints: to see if there were more nudes.

For there was good reason for Murdock's concern. Contrary to the accepted opinion of the general public, he knew that pornography was a much bigger business than the average citizen suspected. There was, it seemed, a wide market for pictures, postcards, films, and obscure, seldom-seen magazines. In spite of the authorities and occasional arrests, the market thrived in some sort of under-the-counter trade, and he understood that the circulation of such things was more or less nation-wide.

Not until he had finished his inspection did he realize he had jumped to a false and unfair conclusion. Already conditioned by a suspicion he was reluctant to admit, he had been afraid that there would be more nudes; that somehow Stacy had been using his camera as a student or salesman of pornography. Now he knew that this was the only nude, and when he looked at it again he saw that even this was not pornography, but seemed to be a studio picture of a standing woman who had been posed in a graceful but not particularly original way. He had seen similar poses in photographic magazines, and as models for calendar artists, and now he went over to his desk to get a magnifying-glass.

The face was instantly familiar, but it took him a second or two to place it because in this picture it seemed younger. Then he knew that this was the woman in the camel's-hair coat who had come to see Ralph Stacy last night with an envelope in her hand.

When he was sure there was but one negative he put this and the print back in the little envelope. Slipping it into his coat pocket, he picked up the other envelopes and negatives and began to sort them out.

There were perhaps a hundred or more negatives and he knew that it would be an all-day job to make reasonable enlargements. In going through the small prints the first time he had noticed a face or two he recognized and now, wanting only to test a theory which he could no longer ignore, he selected certain of these, intending to use them as a test which was already taking shape in his mind.

One print and matching negative showed a police captain, now retired, coming out of a restaurant in the company of a convicted bookmaker and another man Murdock did not know. This he put aside, as he did another print and negative, this one an infra-red shot which showed a man and a woman at some night-club table. There was another strip of film which seemed to show an automobile accident, and he took this too because he wanted to know why it should be kept. The balance of the negatives and prints he put back in the original envelope.

Moving across the living-room, he opened the door of his darkroom, which stood next to the kitchen and had originally been a small dining-room. Knocking out his pipe, he put on his rubber apron and got out his developing-solution and hypo, prepared his trays. Then, before he started his work, he came back and picked up the telephone, dialing the *Courier's* number and asking for the automobile editor.

"Bert," he said when he had his connection. "Kent Murdock. I need a little help on a thing and I think you can give it to me."

"I can try," said Bert. "What is it?"

"You know who handles Hillmans in town?"

"Sure. Mahady Brothers."

"Well, what I want to know is—who in town has bought a maroon convertible within the past year or so. If anything, it's newer than that."

"It's a good thing you don't want to know about a Ford," Bert said. "A Hillman I should be able to check for you."

"It might have been sold to a woman or at least registered in her name. . . . Call me here, will you?" Murdock said and gave his number.

Back in the darkroom, Murdock cut an 8 x 10 sheet into 4 x 5 pieces and put one of them into his enlarging-easel. Selecting the infra-red negative, he focused with the safe-light on and then made his exposure. When he had the print in the hypo he glanced at it for contrast but waited until he had it washing before he took it out and examined it closely.

What he had was a photograph of a man named Phil Avery who in the past had been highly successful in the manipulation of certain gambling enterprises, both locally and as a member of a syndicate that had operated throughout New England. When state and Congressional investigations made such endeavors risky he had put his profits elsewhere, investing in real estate and other more respectable ventures, though his chief activity at present was the operating of Club Avery, one of the town's larger and better known dining and dancing spots.

In this photograph Avery was not alone. He was sitting on a banquette of some unidentifiable restaurant or night club, a blonde woman some years his junior at his side. In spite of the characteristics of infra-red film and bulbs which distorted somewhat the skin values, Avery's mus-tached face had the loose and sagging look that fre-quently comes to those who have had too much to drink. In addition the blonde had one arm draped about his neck, her free hand holding a glass so Avery could have a sip of her drink. It might have made a good honeymoon picture if the blonde had been Avery's wife.

The sequence of the automobile accident puzzled Mur-dock until he'd made his 4 x 5 prints and had a chance to study them. One frame showed a sedan resting on its side on the curbing of some street. The second frame, taken diagonally from behind, showed another car, also a sedan, with a bent rear fender and a smashed side

window. A man was looking backward from the driver's
seat, but his features as he looked out of the lowered
window were unrecognizable. The third frame showed
the same car from the rear so that its four-number license plate was clearly visible. Now, noting that the
number of the wrecked car was also visible, an idea
came to Murdock and he went back to the telephone,
grateful that he had been able to build up such a wide
and varied acquaintanceship over the years. The friend
he telephoned this time worked for the Department of
Motor Vehicles.

From the prints he had, Murdock could not tell what
year the license plates had been issued, but he was
helped here by the state custom which made it possible
for the same number to be reissued to any driver who
applied early. Nearly everyone who had less than a five-
number plate took advantage of the system year after
year, and in this particular instance both license numbers
were relatively low.

The name of Murdock's friend was Arthur Grady. The
two hadn't met in some time and there were the usual
amenities to be taken care of before Murdock read off
the first number and made his request.

"Can you find out who owns that one, Art?"

"Sure," said Art. "You want to hang on?"

"No," Murdock said, "because I've got another one I
want you to check. You have a record of accidents, don't
you?"

"When they're reported as they should be."

"Okay. Then here's what I want on this second number." Murdock read it off. "This car was involved in an
accident, maybe this year, maybe last year. I want to
know what name the car is registered under and also
the owner of the car which was involved with it and
what the result was."

"You mean, was anybody hurt? That sort of thing?"

Murdock said he wanted to find out everything he could and told Art to call back. He hung up and started for the darkroom to see how his prints were drying, but before he got there the telephone shrilled to call him back.

"On that Hillman," Bert said. "There were only three maroon convertibles sold in the last year and a half. One went to some college kid, the second was delivered to a man named Farmer in Weston, and the third was sold to a Mrs. Randolph Jerome."

"Jerome," said Murdock, finding the name familiar.

"The yachtsman," said Bert, "or whatever you want to call him. In the real-estate business and is commodore of some yacht club down Hingham way. Done some ocean racing. You've probably read about him. . . . Why?" said Bert. "What's it all about?"

"Just trying to check a thing," Murdock said. "It's probably not important," he added, making it sound that way, "but I'll let you know if it is."

He had to wait another five minutes for Art Grady to return his call and by that time his 4 x 5's were dry enough to handle. The three prints of the accident he put in a legal-size envelope together with the strip negative. In a similar envelope he put the negative of Phil Avery, the contact print Stacy had made, and the 4 x 5.

"Here's the dope," said Art. "That first number belongs to Frank Deegan, the lawyer. He's had it for the last thirty years. . . . The second one belongs to a guy in Dorchester named John DeMarco."

"He's the one that had the accident."

"Right. About eighteen months ago. A hit-and-run case. Nobody hurt, but the police never turned up the other driver. . . . Funny thing, though," Art said after a moment's hesitation. "We had a letter from DeMarco later. He said he'd had a note in the mail, an anonymous one, with three hundred bucks in cash enclosed to pay for the damages. The other guy must have got a case of conscience, I guess. That all you want?"

Murdock said that was all, and thanked him, the feeling that this might be his lucky day beginning to reassure him as he went again to the darkroom. When he had rinsed his trays he put his apron aside and came back to the living-room to don his jacket and distribute his envelopes in various pockets, saving the inside one for the bulkier envelope that contained the rest of Stacy's negatives.

10

UNLIKE THE Band Box, which was small and intimate and depended on the excellence of Jack Frost's trio, plus a featured entertainer, to attract its customers, the Club Avery offered a sizable dance floor, a twelve-piece band, and a floor show. There was a three-dollar minimum, which went to four on Fridays and Saturdays, but since this could be spent on food as well as drink the club did a good business—often a capacity business—not only with diners and dancers, but with the better-heeled supper trade.

When Kent Murdock arrived at one thirty after having stopped only long enough to get a bowl of soup and a sandwich, the foyer was empty and he stood a moment to let his eyes accustom themselves to the gloomy and unlit interior. He could make out the glass signs on the rest rooms on his left, and opposite them was the long narrow room which made up the bar and cocktail lounge and was aptly termed, by virtue of its wall decorations, the Zebra Room. The tables and chairs had been cleaned out while two men waxed the floor, but they paid no

attention to him as he continued on to the main room
which looked somewhat shoddy and uninviting in the
absence of the artificial lighting under which it thrived.

On the bandstand at the far end the orchestra men,
apparently just winding up a rehearsal, were packing
their instruments, and Murdock continued down the left
side of the room to a corridor, turning right presently
and mounting a flight of stairs. Another corridor leading
to the dressing-rooms opened on the right, but the door
he wanted was just beyond the landing and straight
ahead, a solid-looking door, unadorned and constructed
of gray metal.

Murdock rapped it with his knuckles. A voice called:
"Come in," and then he was in a low-ceilinged office
tastefully furnished in walnut and green leather. The
top of the desk was inlaid with the same kind of leather
that made up the chairs and divan, but at the moment it
was well covered with a widespread copy of the *Morning Telegraph* and a *Scratch Sheet*.

Phil Avery allowed himself a few more seconds of
calculation before he glanced up; then he leaned back,
a lean, medium-sized man of indeterminate age with a
hard, unsmiling face and shrewd black eyes that seldom
revealed more than he wanted them to reveal. He wore
a small black mustache that he kept carefully trimmed
and his straight black hair was shiny with hair tonic
but there was no gray in it. He looked manicured, bar-
bered, scented, and sun-lamped, and his light-gray suit
had been fashioned by an expert.

"Hello, Murdock," he said without enthusiasm. "I've
just been reading about your man Stacy. Too bad, hunh?"

Murdock made no reply. He already had made up his
mind what he wanted to do, and now he took an envelope
from his pocket, removing the contents to make sure he
had the right one. Leaning forward, he arranged the
miniature film, the contact print, and the 4 x 5 on the

open newspaper; then stepped back to perch on the arm of a chair.

Avery gave them little more than a glance. He inspected Murdock with a stare that was hard and bright behind the drooping lids. He had a pencil in one hand, and now he used the point to brush the negative and prints toward Murdock.

"I bought those once before," he said bleakly. "About a year ago. I told Stacy then that there would be no second payment."

He put the pencil down and leaned back again, folding his arms and sticking his chin in the angle made by one thumb and forefinger. Murdock said nothing because he felt a little sick now that he was sure that the thing he feared most was true. While he tried to make the necessary mental adjustment he heard Avery continue.

"I don't know you too well," Avery said. "But I get around and I hear things. The word I got was that you were a leveler, a right one." He grunted offensively. "So I heard wrong. Stacy gets knocked off last night and this morning you're around trying to get a bite for yourself. What happened? Did you inherit the stuff or were you working with him all the time?"

"Wait a minute," Murdock said, the anger rising swiftly at the accusation.

"Take 'em," Avery said. "I wouldn't give you fifteen cents for the three of 'em." His glance slid past Murdock as a door closed. "Show Mr. Murdock the way out," he said.

Murdock glanced over his shoulder as he heard the sound of the door. It was not the one he had entered, but when he saw the two men advance slowly he realized that Avery had signaled them with some push-button concealed in the desk.

"Escort him downstairs," Avery said. "Take him out the back way. And when you get to the alley bounce him

just once; not too hard, but bounce him. You know what
I mean?"

Murdock sat right where he was, shifting his feet
slightly as he remained on the chair arm. They were still
moving toward him, hard-faced, arrogant, sure of themselves, both wearing double-breasted blue suits. One was
about Murdock's size and build with an oblong face and
oversized ears; the other was an inch taller and fifty
pounds heavier, a balding, thick-bodied man with a
crooked nose and brows warped by scar tissue.

"I haven't finished," Murdock said tightly, turning
back to Avery.

"Oh, yes, you have. . . . Okay, boys."

When the hand touched his shoulder Murdock knew
without looking that it was the big man, and the instant
the pressure was applied he lost his temper. It was a
thing that seldom happened to him and came not from
any thought of Stacy or what he might have done but
from the simple fact that Avery had, in effect, called
him a blackmailer without giving him a chance to explain.

"I didn't come here to collect," he snapped. "I came to
find out—"

That was as far as he got. The hand, bunching the
shoulder of his suit and coat, was lifting him. Murdock
moved with it, outraged and furious at the injustice being
done him and not particularly caring what happened
next.

He did not consider the odds, or stop to think that
what he was doing was silly. He knew only that the big
man had the sloping shoulders of a hooker and that he
had to be taken quickly or not at all, and so he brought
his fist around from behind his back and swung, putting
every ounce of weight behind the punch and aiming for
a spot just below the man's breastbone.

He did not punch, actually, but slugged, and he had

the advantage of surprise, and the result was beautiful to behold.

The big man staggered back a step and said: "Ooooo!" His mouth hung open as he gasped for breath and his face took on a greenish cast. He sank down on his knees and, still gasping, tipped slowly over on his side, bent double now as his hands folded across his middle.

Murdock, carried forward by the momentum of the punch and trying to turn, never saw the blow that exploded high up on his jaw. It did not stun him, but his knees buckled and suddenly one of them hit the floor with a jolt that jarred his neck. He bounced up instantly and as he stepped back to give himself fighting room Avery yelled.

"All right!" he said. "That's enough. . . . Felix!"

Felix had his left cocked and he dropped it with reluctance. He stepped back, his grin mean-looking and fixed.

"Give Louie a hand," Avery said. "Get out—both of you."

He turned to Murdock, a curious gleam in his eyes.

"Maybe I was a little hasty," he said. "When I saw these pictures I got sore. You sort of blew your top, didn't you? You couldn't drop Louie like that once in fifteen times."

Murdock felt his muscles relax as the anger left him. He was still breathing hard and it surprised him a little to see the dip of Avery's mustache, to realize the mouth beneath it held a small smile. Behind him he heard the others leave the room, so he again perched on the chair arm.

"You said you didn't come here to collect," Avery said. "You came to find out something. What?"

"I've already found it out," Murdock said. "You told me you paid off Stacy. That's all I want to know."

"What about these?" Avery indicated the negative and prints.

"That's up to you. If they were mine I'd burn them."

Avery picked up the larger print. "Jesus," he said, "a guy can be an awful chump, can't he?" He took out a gold lighter and flicked flame from it. He put the prints and negative in an oversized ash tray and watched them burn.

"Thanks," he said. "Not that they mean anything any more."

Murdock stood up and checked the shape of his hat. As he put it on he thought of something else.

"Did Stacy approach you within the last few days?"

"No. He knew better." Avery leaned back, still watching the flames die out. "I'll tell you about it," he said. "At the time Stacy took that picture—and I'll be damned if I know how or just when he took it—the wife and I had separated. A divorce was cooking and the lawyers were working out a settlement. Stacy came around and we dickered and I finally paid him five hundred bucks because I knew if my wife ever got a look at me the way I was that night with that blonde tramp the alimony and settlement money would have been upped plenty. Now that picture don't mean a thing and Stacy knew it. I should have listened to you before I jumped the gun, should've known you'd never work that kind of a chisel. . . . How about a drink?"

Murdock said he would take a rain check and Avery walked to the door with him. "I'll speak to my maître de," he said. "The next time you come in it's on the house. Bring a friend. . . ."

Frank Deegan had a suite of offices on Federal Street and when Murdock sent his name in he was shown into a huge, paneled room with book-lined walls on two sides. Here the chairs and divan were done in red leather, and the wall-to-wall carpet felt like a well-kept green on a seaside golf course. The top of the massive desk was bare and behind it, in his high-backed chair, sat Frank Deegan.

Deegan had, in years past, been a pretty fair criminal lawyer. The firm he headed was still active in the city and county courts, but in recent years Deegan himself had become more active in politics than in law, though he held no political office. He was a big man physically, with an overfed look about him, and this bulk was at present clothed in a dark-blue suit with a thin line of white piping on the V of his vest. His voice was hoarse and hearty, his chins were three in number, and his florid cheeks were mottled here and there with ruptured veins, as was his prominent nose.

"I've got an appointment in five minutes, Murdock," he said. "What's on your mind?"

Murdock took out the proper envelope, but, with his experience with Avery still fresh in his mind, he did not present it. He clasped his hands behind his back and selected another opening gambit.

"Did you know Ralph Stacy?"

"I knew of him."

"You know what happened last night?"

"Sure, I read the *Courier*."

"Had he been in to see you recently?"

"Here? No."

"In other words," said Murdock, proceeding on the assumption that his theory was correct, "you only paid him off once?"

"Paid him off?" Deegan said, asperity showing in his hoarse voice. "For what?"

"That accident you had last year."

"What accident?" Deegan let his chair tilt forward. "You've lost me somewhere, Murdock," he said, his face inscrutable. "Give me a chance to tune in again."

Murdock put the envelope on the desk. Deegan's gaze remained while his fat fingers fumbled to open it. When he had the strip of negative and the prints on the desk he looked down at them; then he reached down and opened the top drawer on the right.

Murdock waited, his angular face set and shiny and his dark eyes steady. He prepared himself mentally, not knowing what happened next but getting ready for the same sort of treatment—with possible legal refinements —that he had received from Phil Avery. Instead Deegan pulled out an expensive-looking perfecto, bit off one end, and spat the tip on the floor.

"Sit down, Murdock," he said. "Pull up a chair."

Murdock relaxed somewhat. He reached for the indicated chair and pulled it up to the end of the desk.

"What are these pictures for?" Deegan asked.

"They're a present from me to you."

"Where'd you get them?"

"Does it matter?"

"Now that you mention it, no." Deegan examined his cigar, but did not bother to light it. "I just want to be sure you understand that, as of now, these pictures'll get you in more trouble than they will me."

"Unless," said Murdock, bluffing now, "Lieutenant Bacon down at Homicide figures you might possibly have killed Stacy to shut him up."

"That's a possibility. But a remote one."

"Very remote," Murdock said. "I merely presented it as a possibility."

"You have some theory on that accident?"

"I *know* what happened," Murdock said. "One night last year you ran into a man named DeMarco—or he ran into you—and for some reason of your own you decided not to stop. Later you sent him three hundred in cash to pay for the damage to his car. Ralph Stacy just happened to come along at the right time. He took three fast shots with his Leica—you must have seen the flash-bulbs go off—and instead of turning the pictures into the *Courier*, he came to you first."

"I'll be damned," Deegan said, a note of respect in his voice. "You happen to be one-hundred-per-cent right." He paused, his face tightening. "Did Stacy tell you this? How did you happen to—"

Murdock cut him off. He did not want to talk about Stacy. "The answer's right there in those pictures," he said, "for anybody who wants to figure it out."

Deegan leaned back again, his fingers drumming on the desk top. "I didn't have much choice that night," he said reminiscently. "I was driving along, not too fast, and this bastard shoots out of the side street—you can see from the picture that he hit me on the left rear fender—and comes all the way across the street and smacks me." His glance came back to Murdock. "You know why I didn't stop?"

"Drunk?"

"Nope."

"You had somebody with you that you were afraid—"

"Exactly," said Deegan. "I knew if I was caught later I'd lose my driver's license for a year and probably have to pay a fine in traffic court. But if I'd stopped then and word got around who was with me—" He shrugged and cleared his throat. "It wasn't a woman," he said. "But I was in the middle of something big then and it would have been bad—very bad."

"Stacy didn't know who was with you, did he?"

"Fortunately, no. He came around two days later and I thought it would be smarter then to pay him off—I gave him four hundred—than to appear in court and lose my license. I sent DeMarco the money to get the matter off my conscience. I'd been damned lucky and I didn't mind paying a bit for it."

Murdock stood up and buttoned his coat, feeling no

satisfaction in knowing that he had been right, wishing somehow that there might have been some other answer both here and with Phil Avery. He had one more picture to deliver and, though he knew the answer would be the same in so far as Stacy's blackmail activities went, there might in that case be some connection between the blackmail and the murder.

"Is it your idea," Deegan said, "that Stacy might have been shot because of some other pictures he took?"

"I don't know," Murdock said. "I haven't even got an idea and I'm not sure the police have. I happened to run across some of Stacy's films and I wanted to find out how he operated."

"I don't imagine you'll be spreading the news," Deegan said. "Well, neither will I."

Murdock said he was counting on that. He put his hat on and went out while Deegan began again to examine the present Murdock had brought him.

11

THE RIVERSIDE was one of the newer and more expensive apartment houses that had in recent years been erected in the so-called Kenmore Square district. Constructed of rough-textured brick, it boasted a marquee, heavy glass doors, and a sedate but attractive lobby done in black and white. There was no doorman in sight when Murdock arrived, but there was a clerk in attendance behind the small desk opposite the two elevators.

He looked up from his accounts as Murdock stopped to ask the number of Randolph Jerome's apartment. He asked if Murdock was expected and Murdock lied cheerfully by saying that he had just telephoned Mrs. Jerome.

He was aware of the other's quick but expert appraisal, and apparently the clerk decided Murdock looked sufficiently prosperous and well dressed to warrant admission.

"6-B," he said, and turned back to his accounts.

The elevator was quiet, its operator ancient. "On your right, sir," he said when the door swung silently back.

There were four apartments on the floor and 6-B was on the left rear, giving its tenants a river view. A colored maid opened the door in answer to his ring and he asked her to tell Mrs. Jerome that Mr. Murdock was here.

"She's not expecting me," he said, "but I think she'll see me. Mr. Murdock, from the *Courier*."

The maid let him in but left him in the foyer and while he waited he moved in front of the mirror to smooth down his hair and check the knot in his tie. He took off his balmacaan and folded it on the chair next to the oblong table. He approved of the gray Shetland suit he wore, but he did not care much for the face that looked back at him. It looked tired and depressed, the mouth compressed unpleasantly and the eyes sullen. He flexed it deliberately in an effort to wipe out the tightness and found he could twist the mouth into something that could pass for a smile. He did not hear Mrs. Jerome coming until she spoke to him from the living-room doorway.

"Hello, Mr. Murdock."

Her voice was pleasantly husky, as he had remembered it, and her green-eyed glance was direct but not hostile. She wore gray slacks which were neatly pressed, well fitted, and properly hung. On her they looked very well indeed, as did the thin, black, turtle-neck sweater. Remembering the nude photograph, and seeing her now, he was aware that she still had the sort of erect and firmly rounded figure that any woman would envy. The unaffected way she stood there gave him the idea that she was well aware of this and proud of the fact. When he stepped forward to meet her she surprised him by offering her hand and shaking his firmly.

"Come in, won't you?" she said. "I've been rather expecting you, but I'd be interested to know how you found me."

She led the way into a modern-looking room that at first glance seemed mostly windows and mirrors. One corner was picture glass for a view of the river, the furniture was in blond wood, the oversized divan looked custom-made, and the rug felt like foam rubber underfoot. There were a Renoir over the fireplace and two Goya etchings of bullfight scenes over the divan.

"Sit down," she said. "Would you like a drink?"

Murdock thanked her and said it was a little early for him. He sat down on one end of the divan at her silent direction, still surprised at her easy, matter-of-fact manner and his curiosity mounting.

"What made you think I'd be around?" he asked.

"Oh, I don't know." She waved one arm, and bracelets jangled on her wrist. "You looked like an intelligent man, and you're a newspaperman, and newspapermen are supposed to be clever. In my mind it was just a question of who would be here first, you or the police. I imagine you told them about me? . . . What exactly did you tell them?" she said as Murdock nodded.

"I told Lieutenant Bacon you were a knockout—"

"Thank you."

"—with reddish-brown hair, a lovely complexion, and an expensive camel's-hair coat. I said you had an envelope in your pocket. Bacon asked me to classify you and I told him that as a guess I'd say you were either married to, or being kept by, a gentleman of means."

Her green eyes suggested that she was pleased at what she had heard and her sense of humor brought a twist to her red mouth. By that time Murdock was convinced that her grooming, make-up, assurance, and directness of manner could only have come with long practice. This woman was no amateur, and he discovered that he liked her very much indeed.

"How *did* you find me?" she asked.

"I saw you drive up," Murdock said. "It wasn't hard to check on a maroon Hillman convertible, Mrs. Jerome."

"Let's not be so formal," she said. "The name is Vivian, and yours is Kent, I believe, and how come the police haven't been able to check the Hillman?"

Murdock grinned. He said he had forgotten to describe the Hillman.

"On purpose?"

"I don't think so, but I wouldn't swear to it."

"So what happens now?"

"I don't know," Murdock said and produced the negative and prints for her inspection.

She picked up the 4 x 5 print and looked at it a long time, turning it this way and that to get it in the proper light. When she glanced at him her eyes were no longer amused and her tone was curt and disgusted.

"I suppose you have others, like Stacy had. How many more are there, for God's sake?"

"That's all of them."

"I thought I bought all there were the first time."

"When?"

"Six or seven months ago. I gave him five hundred dollars and he gave me the negative. Then the day before yesterday—" She broke off, her frown warping the well-kept brows. "How did he get this other film?"

"One way," Murdock said, "would be to make a good enlargement and photograph that. That would give him a second negative, maybe not quite so good as the first but good enough. . . . What happened the day before yesterday?"

She stretched to one side, back arched and breasts lifting as she reached for a cigarette box on the end table. She offered it to Murdock and he moved closer and took one. When she had her light she tucked one sandaled foot under her and blew smoke at the ceiling; then she eyed him directly, her face otherwise expressionless.

"For over three years I've been married to what you might call an aristocrat, assuming you're the sort who admits there are such things. His friends are like he is, a cut or so above the crowd I used to run with. I like them and I can talk their language now without thinking twice about it. But sometimes I'd rather not. Sometimes I like to let go and say what I please, and in my own uncultured way. This is going to be one of those times because I'm in no mood for polished repartee."

She paused, her eyes busy but no longer distressed. "I was plenty worried last night. I didn't know who you were at first and I didn't know what to do, but you made an impression just the same. I don't know whether it was your looks, or the way you wore your clothes, or the way you talked. Call it intuition, if you like, but you seemed like a right guy to me. You still do. So what I want to know before we talk about the day before yesterday is, are you going to cover for me with the police?"

"Not exactly," Murdock said.

"What do you mean, not exactly?"

"With the picture, yes. I think that's the only negative and now it's yours."

As he spoke she folded the 4 x 5 print, put it with the contact print and negative, thrust all three into the pocket of her slacks. "Well," she said, letting her breath come out, "that's something anyway."

"The police will probably find you themselves, but whether they do or not I'll probably tell Bacon I found out who you were. He'll want to know how and I'll have to tell him about the Hillman. He'll be around and he'll say that I say you were at Stacy's last night and he'll ask why and you'll tell him Stacy was blackmailing you—"

"Suppose I just tell him you're a liar and that I wasn't there at all."

Murdock examined her with one eye and then with both.

"Well, you can try that too."

"And if I don't?"

"Then Bacon'll want to know what Stacy was black-mailing you for and you can tell him it's none of his business, or you can say it was a picture and let it go at that. So far as I know, you've got the only negative and you and I are the only ones who know there ever was such a thing."

"Amen," she said dryly. "Then that makes me a suspect."

"You were there," Murdock said. "For all I know, you could have gone there with a gun."

"What makes you think so?"

"The way you kept your right hand tucked in your pocket."

Something flickered in her glance and was quickly gone as she picked a piece of loose tobacco from her lower lip.

"I had five hundred bucks tucked in that envelope too," she said.

Murdock, remembering that envelope and watching her closely now, had the feeling that she was telling the truth.

"The police found the envelope," he said. "They didn't find the money."

She made no reply to this. She jabbed her cigarette into an ash tray and studied her red-painted nails.

"You're making it rough for me," she said.

"I could have gone to Bacon first with the photograph."

"That's right, you could." She hesitated, frown fixed. Then she glanced up. "Look! If I tell you the story of that photo, will you have to tell the police?"

"No," Murdock said. "All I have to tell them is that you're the woman who came to Stacy's and was there when I left."

"Fair enough," she said, and smiled. "Sit back, Kent. Relax. This'll take a while. . . . Sure you won't change your mind about that drink?"

She turned from the hips and put one arm along the back of the divan. "That picture was taken about five years ago. In a Chicago studio. And the funny part of it is that I didn't know it had been taken; didn't even know it was in existence until seven or eight months ago.

"I was a model at the time," she said. "Fashions mostly, but not the high-fashion sort of thing because I was never quite skinny enough for that. And sometimes things got tough all over and I'd take a job for an artist or illustrator, provided he was recommended by someone I knew." She paused again, her smile ingenuous and her green gaze amused.

"Remember the publicity about that girl in Hollywood who posed for some calendar art before she got in the movies? Well, this was the same sort of deal. The photograph was for an artist who had a calendar assignment. The body was for him and he was supposed to glamorize it and put a pretty face on it. So I posed and Ralph Stacy, who was a friend of this photographer, walked in. I didn't even know he was there at first because the floods were on and I couldn't see anything beyond them. Later when we had finished I saw he had a little camera, but what I didn't know was that he'd snapped a couple of exposures while the other picture was being taken, using the same lights."

She grunted contemptuously, an unladylike sound. "Don't ask me what he wanted with them—maybe he collected nudes—or why he kept them all those years. But he did, and since then I've done all right for myself.

I came east and worked in New York for a while, and I had a friend up here who had opened a high-priced shop down on Newbury Street. She talked me into coming up to help her and that's where I was when Randy came in with his sister. I guess you know he was a widower. He has a son in Texas in the air corps and—"

She stopped short. "It doesn't matter how I met Randy. The point is he fell in love with me and we were married and then one day Stacy, who was now working for the *Courier,* saw me or found out who I was—I'm not even sure about that—and called me up. He said he had a photograph I ought to see and he told me just enough to make me curious. I agreed to meet him. He told me how and when he took the picture—not that it mattered, because there it was."

"You paid him five hundred dollars for the negative and print," Murdock said. "You figured that wrapped it up? That's all there was to it?"

"Well—not quite all. Once he had the money, he made another little pitch. He said his wife was looking for a part-time job and she'd had office experience and would I mind asking my husband if he could find a place for her."

Murdock's mind came quickly to attention. Mrs. Stacy working for Randolph Jerome? Did Bacon know this?

"Was there a place?" he asked, unable to wait for the finish of the story.

"Yes. A week later, that is. I spoke to Randy and he said he might be able to use some extra help and—well, she's been there ever since. I understand Randy is quite pleased with her work."

Murdock let it go at that because right now he could not tell whether this information had any significance or not and there were other things he had to know.

"Okay," he said. "So the day before yesterday Stacy got in touch with you again."

"In a letter. It came in the morning. There was a little photo inside and a typewritten, unsigned note which said there was one more negative for sale at the same price as the first one, that I was to wait for a phone call."

She swung her arm down, her sleek brows furrowing again and no longer looking at Murdock.

"It scared me at first because I didn't understand how there could be another negative, and then I got so damn mad I almost went to Randy and told him the whole story. The picture had been taken a long time ago and I'd done nothing to be ashamed of, actually; it was just a job I needed and—well, all of that was true and still I knew it would be better if Randy didn't know."

"What did Stacy say when he called?"

"Just what you'd expect. I hadn't made up my mind then and I tried to bluff him by saying if he ever sent a picture to my husband Randy would probably beat hell out of him—and I think he would," she added honestly. "But Stacy said he wouldn't have to send a print to Randy. He said some of my friends might just happen to get one of the prints anonymously."

She hesitated again and now her voice grew quietly intent. "I've been damned lucky with Randy. I think we've got about as close to a happy marriage as you'll find. Maybe not in that adolescent, romantic way you read about in the magazines, but he loves me just the same. He thinks I'm wonderful and he seems proud to be seen with me, and, speaking for myself, I know I've made him happy. I like what I have and I'd fight for it if I had to. It's a pretty solid partnership and, while I think Randy would understand about that picture, I still had to ask myself whether it was worth taking a chance of—well, disillusioning him, even a little bit. . . . So," she said, "I decided to play along one more time. I went down to the bank and got five hundred in new fifties. I'd told Stacy I'd bring it to him last night."

She stopped, as though that was the end of the story. She folded her arms, unconsciously bunching her breasts, brooding silently over her thoughts as she looked fixedly across the room. Murdock waited, thinking now, finding her story convincing on the whole but understanding too that she had offered no proof that she had not killed Stacy.

For here was a woman who was wise and experienced in many things. She had said she would fight for what she had and he believed her, knowing that her achievements were hers alone and came as no accident of birth or inheritance. She had gone to see Stacy with the money. She had given him the money. But that, Murdock knew, did not prove her innocent. She still could have taken a gun. She could have threatened Stacy, who might have been foolish enough to laugh at her, to taunt her, to try to bluff things out. Under the proper circumstances she could have fired and, in the shock and panic that came with the act, have kept on firing, fleeing when sanity returned without bothering about the money she had brought or even thinking about it.

"You gave him the money," he said, picking out the obvious hole in her story, "but you didn't get the negative."

"No, I didn't." She moistened her lips and said: "I'll tell you why. I'd bought one negative. He gypped me on that and if he was that kind of guy he could keep on gypping me. For all I knew, he might have three or four more negatives. I wanted him to understand that I didn't care about the picture. I was paying him one more time to keep his mouth shut and leave me alone, and if he ever tried again—"

"In other words, you threatened him?"

"Yes, I suppose I did."

Murdock thought of saying: "With a gun?" But he
didn't. He nodded, still not sure whether he believed her
or not. He put his palms on his knees. He pushed himself erect, and after a quick curious glance she untangled
her legs and stood beside him. She did not say anything
as he went into the foyer, but went with him and waited
until he had put on his coat. Then she looked up at him,
her green eyes wide and appealing.

"Don't you believe me?" she asked quietly.

"Does it matter?" he said. "You went there. That's all
I know for sure. If you shot him you certainly wouldn't
admit it."

She stood close now, her bosom touching lightly the
front of his coat. She gave him a moment of thoughtful
appraisal; then her red mouth smiled enigmatically.

"I don't suppose there's any way I could lure you into
not going to the police?" She stepped back, tilting her
bobbed head, then answering herself. "No, I suppose
there isn't. . . . Well, thanks for the picture, anyway."

She offered her hand again and he held it a moment,
feeling the magnetism of her personality and her physical nearness.

"If you read the paper," he said, "you know the police
are looking for a woman in a camel's-hair coat. Maybe
it would be a good idea to go see Lieutenant Bacon
and—"

"Tell him I'm the one?" She drew back, frowning
again.

"Why not? You'll find he's a pretty fair-minded guy
and it'll look better that way. Think it over anyway. I
won't be seeing him for a while."

With that he let go of her hand and opened the door,
closing it behind him without looking back.

12

ON THE ride to Jack Frost's place Murdock recapitulated the results he had achieved in the past two hours and discovered that his accomplishments had been two in number. The first was that Ralph Stacy had been using his camera and the entree provided by the *Courier* to blackmail certain individuals over an extended period. The second fact was that of the four cases Murdock knew about, two—Avery and Deegan—had been approached but once, possibly because the photographs were no longer of much value or because Stacy was afraid to go back; with young Hargrove and Vivian Jerome, Stacy had made a second try within the past couple of days. How many other people might have been approached it would be impossible to know without developing the remaining negatives and running down each and every one. It did seem likely, however, that Stacy had made at least one other try; otherwise there would be no explanation for the two hoodlums who had come to his apartment last night to rob the darkroom of its films and, in doing so, knock Mrs. Stacy unconscious.

Murdock took these thoughts with him as he paid off the taxi and climbed the alleylike street which angled steeply upward on the wrong side of the Hill. Here the brick houses were small and ancient, most of them built flush with the sidewalk, their flat roofs mounting upward in broad steps. The narrow-front building he sought had a basement apartment with barred, street-level windows, and three floors over it. Frost occupied the top one and as Murdock climbed the last flight of stairs he could hear the piano.

There was only one door at the landing and Murdock stood there listening; for this was his kind of piano and he did not want to interrupt the full-chorded chorus of "It Had to Be You" that Frost was working over. The left-hand tenths were unusual and the harmonic variations were something that had never been written on paper. But there was a familiarity to the arrangement and now, as the piece ended and he knocked on the door, he knew why.

Jack Frost was wearing a tattered blue bathrobe over his pajamas, a tall, slat-thin man in his early thirties with a stooped, flat-chested look that had been developed by his years of sitting in front of a piano. He had a sad, long-jawed face and sardonic brown eyes and right now his customary night-club pallor was augmented by a stubble of beard.

"Hi, Kent," he said without enthusiasm. "Come in. Sit down if you can find a place."

He went back to the piano bench and picked the cigarette stub from an ash tray, giving it a final drag before crushing it out. Murdock, after a quick look about the crowded, untidy room, distinguished only by the expensive television-radio-record-playing console and a whole wall full of records, lifted a stack of arrangements from a rocker and eased into it.

"I listened to that last chorus outside," he said. "At first I thought it was Tatum."

"Hah!" said Frost. "That'll be the day."

"Where'd you get the arrangement?"

Frost grinned. "From Tatum," he said. "I'll bet I've played that record four hundred times." He shook his head. "But nobody plays like Tatum and don't let anybody tell you anybody's going to replace him. Me, I kick it around in an amateurish sort of way just to see how it comes out. Maybe on any given piece I could fool a lot of people, but not you, pal."

"For eight bars."

"Okay. Eight bars. After that you hear a little thing—maybe only a little thing if I've listened hard—and you say: 'No, that ain't Art.' . . . I've got the hands," he said, "but I still can't get the crispness and nobody's got what he's got in his head: that inventiveness and sense of harmony. And even if you had that much you wouldn't have the technical equipment to bring it off."

"The only thing that burns me," Murdock said as Frost began to finger some chords, "is that you go into a club to hear him and sometimes you have to sit there through two shows to get one piece the way you want it. He plays too much piano, and to me a lot of it seems right-hand crazy."

Frost agreed. "Sure. I know what you like, and I'm with you. But Tatum's probably proud of what he can do and he knows nobody else can do it that way. A lot of it could be mostly done to impress the customers who don't know a third from a seventh, musically speaking. They hear a lot of notes and it's pretty damned amazing, you know that. So they're satisfied they've heard the most, and they have. Also you've got to remember that not everybody likes 'Sweet Lorraine' the way you do."

Murdock grinned at the soundness of Frost's analysis. "Go ahead," he said. "One chorus, now that you've brought it up."

"Like the old record or the newer one?"

"The old one."

"Yeah," said Frost. "I think I like that one best too."

He played it and it was clear that he had practiced it more than once, for it came out relaxed and faithfully copied and very wonderful to hear. Hearing it and watching the nimble fingers, Murdock remembered other things.

As a youth Frost had worked with some of the better name bands and had established himself not only as a

competent pianist but as a capable arranger. To hear him
tell it, he had become fed up with one-night stands and
buses and cheap hotels and the repetitive grind of playing the same arrangements night after night. Also he was
a New Englander by birth, so he had come back to try
his hand at this and that, his technique and understanding of his profession growing all the time until he finally
settled on his own trio and his own arrangements. Visit-
ing band leaders dropped in to hear him when they
could, and he had a weekly fifteen-minute spot on the
radio, with an occasional guest shot now and then. He
continued to play his way and enjoy it. It was unlikely
that he would ever achieve national fame as some with
less equipment had done, and, to Murdock, this refusal
to substitute musical hokum for his own integrity explained why he was working in the Band Box for perhaps
a hundred and a half a week when, with other methods,
he might be making three or four times that much.

Now, as Frost hit his last chord and turned on the
bench to reach for a cigarette, Murdock thanked him.
He said it was great and then, wishing earnestly that he
could hear some more of the same, he cleared his throat
and got ready to change the subject. His intention must
have shown in his face because Frost eyed him narrowly.

"So what the hell did you come here for?" he said.
"Not to hear Tatum. What's on your mind, Dad? Ralph
Stacy?"

"You talked to Bacon?"

"Until about half past three this morning. I only got
up about an hour ago. That's why the costume."

"I understand you got out of line last night."

"Plenty," Frost said. "I can't drink any more. I ought
to know it by now."

"You were going to Stacy's and beat his brains out.
Because he took your girl."

"You're half right. I don't think she was ever my girl. Maybe I only thought she was."

"You got her her job, didn't you?"

"In a way." Frost rubbed his tousled hair and scratched his nape. "I'll tell you about Nancy," he said finally. "She came from out Ohio way. Big family and she wanted to get away. Thought she could sing and managed to hook up with some small combo that was passing through. After that it was mostly road stuff playing dance halls, taverns, cheap clubs, fraternities, banquets, benefits, everything but square dances. She had a couple of years of that and last summer she was up in Maine at a summer spot and when the season ended, the band fell apart."

He paused, his glance remote. "She came in here late one afternoon just as we finished rehearsing. I remember they'd brought 'Maybe' back and we were trying to make it sound like it was Joe Mooney or Page Cavanaugh. I really didn't have any use for a canary, but—I don't know—there was something about her, something appealing. She was cute-looking, and after we'd talked a bit I could tell she wasn't like some of these tough illiterate little monkeys that think they can sing. She named a piece and I asked her what key and we ran through a chorus."

He shrugged. "She couldn't sing much. All right maybe, but not for a spot like the Band Box and not with the kind of p.a. system they've got there. Her phrasing was bad and her voice was small and she was scared and—well, it wasn't worth fooling around with. I told her I didn't think she was ready, but that I understood the hatcheck girl was quitting the end of the week. I said if she needed work I'd speak to the boss, and all he needed was one look at that blond hair and nice figure."

He stopped to light a fresh cigarette from the inch-long butt and Murdock sat motionless lest there be some digression before the story was finished.

"Well, she needed a job," Frost said, "so she took it. And she'd come in the afternoon lots of times to listen to us rehearse. She liked music and she still had this idea about singing and I fooled around with her some, trying to teach her what I could, but it was still nothing but ordinary. Then one day I found out something else— she could play a bit of piano. She was no Mary Lou Williams, or even Barbara Carroll, but it wasn't too bad and we started fooling around.

"I made some arrangements and sometimes I'd take her to the radio station where we could get two pianos. I thought we might work something up and maybe cut a platter or two, maybe get a sustaining spot. We put some stuff on tape and it wasn't too bad and then Stacy started giving her a play." He paused and now the enthusiasm with which he had talked about Tatum was gone and his tone was flat and unemotional.

"He gave her a lot of time and he was a good-looking guy with a lot of clothes and a big car and he started taking her around afternoons and meeting her after we closed. I figured I made as much dough as Stacy—" He looked up, his glance probing. "I never figured you newspaper guys were overpaid, but Stacy had it—and he spent a little of it on her. Also I guess I'm a pretty dull guy once I get out of my groove. Anyway the competition was too tough."

"So last night you got drunk," Murdock said, "and decided to beat him up."

"Yeah," said Frost. "And I should've known better. I got too drunk. I didn't have what it takes." He went on, talking easily now—too easily, Murdock thought—as he related the same account Murdock had heard from Lieutenant Bacon.

"Bacon's wondering if maybe Nancy did the shooting," he said when Frost finished. "He thinks maybe Stacy was getting ready to give her the air."

"That's crazy," Frost protested. "She loved the guy—or thought she did."

"Women have killed men they loved—or thought they did—before."

The telephone rang before Frost could reply and he turned to glare at it. When it rang again he rose and went over to a table that was cluttered with papers, arrangements, music sheets.

"Yeah," he said. "Who?" Then he was listening, his face suddenly grave and disturbed. Twice his troubled glance slid to Murdock and he pulled it back and finally he said: "Look. I'll have to call you back. Yeah . . . What's your number there?"

He reached for a small pad and found a pencil. He grabbed it savagely and his hand was white-knuckled as he wrote hurriedly and hard. He hung up with a bang and tore the sheet from the pad.

"I'm going to have to get on the ball," he said to Murdock. "Have to shave and get cleaned up." He stopped in the doorway of the adjoining bedroom. "See you at the club, hunh?"

He stepped inside then, closing the door after him as Murdock started to button his coat. For another few seconds he stood there frowning, wondering what had brought the sudden change in Frost. Then, prompted by some curiosity he did not try to analyze, he walked over to the table and picked up the pad. Frost had made his notation with considerable pressure and, by holding the pad so he could get a strong cross-light, Murdock could make out the number which had been impressed there.

When he had memorized it he went over to the door, still not knowing what to think. As he went down the stairs he found himself hoping that Frost was not the man who had killed Stacy; there were too few piano players like him left, and too many chordless acrobats left over from the bop school.

It was a simple matter for Kent Murdock to check the number he had memorized, and his quest took him to a downtown street which bisected a neighborhood of small, grubby-looking stores and old loft buildings. The address proved to be little more than a doorway sandwiched between a stationery store and a radio shop which made up the ground floor of an old two-story building flanked by taller ones.

The lettering on the second-floor windows overlooking the street proclaimed to all that here were the offices of the Downtown Loan Company. There was a narrow hall which led from the foyer to a door at the rear, and the stairs mounted straight ahead to a corridor which opened on the left. Murdock started along this, past the various doorways of the loan company, and now a man swung round the corner of the transverse hall which led to the rear.

He wore a brown covert-cloth coat and a brown Homburg, a well-built middle-aged man with a muscular, smooth-shaven face and a worried look in his eye. Had it not been for Murdock's earlier activities he might not have recognized that face, though it probably would have seemed familiar since he had seen pictures of it before. As it was he put a name to the face in that moment when they passed each other. When he started down the corridor on his right he also knew where the man had come from—or thought he did.

For on his immediate left and backing up to the loan company's suite was a frosted-glass door which spoke of the occupancy of: *Albert Vance—Stamps—Bought. Sold. Exchanged.* Extending down the right side were the three-door offices of a cut-rate tailoring establishment. Opposite, and next to the Vance office, was another door which had been lettered to read: *Martin Epps—Private Investigator.* There were two doors here and Murdock opened the one that said: *Enter Here.*

It was a smallish office, sparsely furnished with an oaken settee, two matching chairs, and a table covered with old copies of *Life* and *Look*. There was a hooded typewriter on another table in the corner, but the dust on the cover indicated it had not been used recently.

The connecting door on the right stood open and Murdock could see the desk and the man behind it, who watched as Murdock approached but made no move. Sitting down, he looked tall and thin and flat-chested, like Jack Frost, but instead of being stooped he had a pod which started at his belt line and extended downward.

"Come in, mister," he said, and waved at the straight-backed chair at the end of the desk.

The office was as dusty as the anteroom but more crowded. There were two metal filing-cabinets, a water-cooler, a sectional bookcase, mostly empty. The one sooty window looked out on a brick wall punctured by other similar windows.

Murdock fanned out his coat and sat down, aware now that Martin Epps was about forty, an inconspicuous-looking man with mousy brown hair, a sallow complexion, and stained, irregular teeth. His nose was long and thin and his amber-colored eyes were quick and slyly observant.

"Do I know you from somewhere?" he said.

"Murdock," Murdock said. "The *Courier*."

"Yeah," said Epps. "Heard of you." He grinned. "You got a problem? Trouble with your wife?"

Murdock lit a cigarette and when he finished Epps leaned forward to borrow the burning match. When he had his own cigarette going he threw the match on the floor and hooked his thumbs in the pockets of his un-bottoned vest.

"I've got a problem all right," Murdock said. "What I want to know is why you were parked outside Ralph Stacy's place last night."

"What?"

"I passed you on the street just after you'd left the corner drugstore."

If Epps was startled he did not show it. He peered at Murdock like a nearsighted man who had forgotten his glasses. After three seconds of that he flicked ashes on the floor and leaned back.

"Not me, brother," he said flatly.

"About ten twenty or so," Murdock said. "You followed that maroon Hillman and you parked across the street." He hesitated, a feeling of annoyance stirring inside when he got no reaction. "I just passed Randolph Jerome in the hall, and I don't think he was buying stamps or ordering a suit from that outfit across the hall."

"You got a theory on that Stacy job? . . . Because if you have," Epps said, "maybe we can crack it together." He paused, his amber gaze innocent and amused. "I understand there's maybe going to be a reward. I could use some of it."

Murdock understood he was being kidded, but he kept the irritation from coloring his words.

"I think Jerome hired you to tail his wife yesterday," he said. "You followed her to Stacy's, waited outside a minute, and then went across the street to see who lived there. I think you went down to the drugstore to phone Jerome and break the news and then you went back to wait in your car. When I left you were still there and she was in Stacy's place. She was still there when Stacy came back, because the envelope she brought for him was found by the police. . . . Are you with me so far?" he added evenly.

"I'm getting your message," Epps said. "You're coming through loud and clear. The trouble is you're talking about some other guy."

"So maybe she killed him," Murdock said, ignoring the comment. "Or maybe she left and Jerome came to hear what you had to say. If he got that far he might have gone over to see who was bothering his wife, and why. He could have gone up there and got himself in a hassle. Or maybe you went up to have a look—"

"Sorry, keed." Epps shook his head. "The partnership deal is off. I can't buy any of that, so you work your way and I'll work mine."

Murdock reached forward and pulled the telephone across the desk. He dialed a number and when he had an answer he asked for Lieutenant Bacon. As he did so Epps swore and came upright in his chair to slap a finger across the receiver bar and break the connection.

For a moment then they eyed each other, neither moving. Murdock waited, angular face tight and his dark gaze menacing. When Epps kept the pressure on the finger, he lifted the handset and swung it at the detective's wrist. Epps swore and yanked his hand to safety.

"What's the idea?" Murdock said. "Why the hell should I go down the street to a pay station when I can phone here for nothing?"

Epps measured Murdock's challenge, considered the thin, unpleasant grin. He was still weighing the odds when Murdock started to dial again. Apparently Epps did care for those odds, because this time there was no interruption and Murdock identified himself when he heard Bacon's voice.

"Do you know a private dick named Martin Epps?" he asked.

"Know of him," Bacon said. "A cheap subpoena server who works mostly on divorce cases."

"Epps is the guy I saw last night," Murdock said, and went on to refresh Bacon's memory as to the circumstances.

"The one that tailed the dame and parked across the street?" Bacon said. "You sure? How do you know?"

"Does it matter? He'll probably deny it, but I thought

you might want to work him over and see what he says."

Epps had shifted his gaze to the sooty window and now he sat that way, his mouth mean and only the lips moving. He was cursing softly and steadily when Murdock hung up and the cursing followed Murdock out of the office and clear across the anteroom.

13

THE BUILDING where Randolph Jerome had his office was less than a block away, but on an intersecting street where the atmosphere was more prosperous. This door on the fifth floor was lettered to read: *Randolph Jerome—Real Estate,* and when Murdock entered he found himself in an L-shaped anteroom extending round the partitioned private office in the corner. There were several green metal filing-cabinets in the anteroom, and two desks. The one by the window, apparently Elinor Stacy's, was unoccupied; at the other a pleasant-man-nered brunette stopped beating the typewriter and stood up to see what Murdock wanted. When he told her she went into the private office and then, a moment later, came out to hold the door open.

"You can go right in, Mr. Murdock," she said with a smile.

Randolph Jerome's office was conservatively furnished, as the man himself was dressed. He sat behind a mod-est-sized desk, a prosperous-looking figure in his early fifties, clad in a three-button dark-brown suit. There was a glow of health in his full-fleshed cheeks and a lingering tan that might have come from Florida or from the out-door work he had been doing on his ketch. His thin, sandy hair was graying and he had a way of speaking that, in some, would have sounded somewhat stilted.

There was, Murdock knew, a reason for this. For Jerome was not a self-made man. He came from a good family, he had been properly educated, with some time abroad after college, and his affluence was inherited, his real-estate business consisting mostly of the management of property he owned. This gave him the time he desired for his yachting activities, and it seemed unlikely that he would ever be in need of social security when he became sixty-five. Now he watched Murdock advance, unsmiling, his blue eyes fixed but not hostile and giving no indication that he had seen Murdock twenty minutes earlier.

"Yes, Mr. Murdock," he said. "You're from the *Courier*?"

"But not on *Courier* business," Murdock said, deciding that it would do no good to fence verbally with this man. "I just came from Martin Epps's office. I passed you in the hall as I went in."

Jerome neither affirmed nor denied the statement. He said: "Sit down, won't you? . . . Now, what is it you wish to talk about?"

"About Ralph Stacy, mostly."

"Oh, yes." Jerome nodded thoughtfully. "I read about that. He was from the *Courier* too, I believe." He rocked in his chair and then he frowned, his gaze intent. "And is it your thought that this concerns me in some way?"

Murdock returned his gaze with steady eyes. He did not like what he was doing, but he knew of no other way, and during the past hours his patience had been wearing thin. Bluntly, but as pleasantly as he could, he said:

"You're probably busy, Mr. Jerome. I know I am. We're not going to get anywhere by being obscure with each other, so let's forget it. I think you hired Martin

Epps to follow your wife. If you did, you know she went
to see Ralph Stacy last night."

He saw Jerome's face tighten and spoke quickly to cut
him off. "Let's not kid about it. I know she was there. I
left her in Stacy's apartment. I know Epps's car was
parked across the street and I saw him come out of the
corner drugstore. My thought on that is that he telephoned you when he found out where she went."

He swallowed, knowing he was on thin ice now, just
as Stacy had been on thinner ice for a long time. He had
no idea whether Jerome knew about the picture or not,
but he had to find out.

"I don't know what happened after that, but I think
Epps does, and maybe you do. I also think I ought to tell
you that I know about the picture that has been worrying your wife."

"Picture?"

"The one taken some years back when she was a
model."

He had his reaction then. Jerome slid his forearms
across the desk, his face hard and mouth tight. There
was a glint in the blue eyes that gave him the look of a
battler, and it seemed to Murdock that here was a man
who could be a tough adversary and a hard one to whip.

"Just how," he said coldly, "do you know about that
picture, Mr. Murdock?"

"I'll tell you," Murdock said. "But I'd like a little ex-
change of information if you don't mind. If you killed
Stacy—and on the face of it that is not so absurd as it
may seem—you're certainly not going to admit it. If
your wife did, you're going to cover up for her. Short of
those two alternatives, there are some things I want to
know. . . . I got the picture of your wife from some
films Stacy had left hidden in a bookcase," he said and
then explained the circumstances.

"Where is that picture now?" Jerome demanded, still on the offensive.

"I gave it to your wife. By now I imagine she's destroyed it."

"Does she have any idea that I know about it?"

"No."

"Or that you planned to come to see me?"

"I didn't have the idea myself until I saw you in that building around the corner."

Jerome leaned back, a change coming gradually over his attitude and appearance. When he spoke again his cultured accent had the sound of a man whose thoughts had gone a long way back.

"I found out about the picture the day before yesterday," he said. "That night, rather. The letter came in the morning. Vivian opened it at breakfast and I could tell by her reaction that she was seriously disturbed, even though at the time I had no idea what the letter was about. I wouldn't have known at all except for the sheerest of accidents."

He reached for a brass letter opener and began to finger it absently. "That night I woke up, an unusual thing in itself, and when I could not get back to sleep I got up to get a cigarette. Not wanting to wake my wife, I went into the living-room and began looking through the various cigarette boxes, all of which were empty. Now, Vivian smokes as much as I do, or more, and when I saw her handbag I opened it to see if she had a package. The bag was rather full of the things that women carry, and in rummaging around in it I inadvertently dropped the envelope. It had been opened at one end and it hit the floor in such a way that the little photograph slid out along with a portion of an enclosed sheet."

He sighed softly and his glance came back to Murdock. "I couldn't help seeing the picture. It startled me,

so I took it over to the light for a better look and then
I knew beyond all doubt that Vivian had posed for it.
Then I did something I'd never done before in my life,
a thing I make no attempt to excuse or justify. . . . I
looked at the enclosure," he said quietly. "Then I went
back to bed and thought about it until morning."

"You knew your wife had been a model, didn't you?"
Murdock asked.

"Certainly. The photograph in itself meant nothing to
me; by that I mean it did not bother me. I could tell it
had been taken some years ago and what happened in
those days was no concern of mine. I didn't know who
had sent that letter. What I did deduct from its wording
was the fact that Vivian had been blackmailed and had
paid for a duplicate photograph at some time in the past;
that this was a fresh demand for more money.

"Now I have no intention of discussing my marital
affairs with you," he said, "except to say that this second
venture of mine has been a most happy one in every possible way. I love my wife and I know she respects me,
and the important thing to me is that nothing happen
to change the balance of this relationship, not even a
little. If you can understand this you may also understand that I did not want my wife to know that *I knew*
about that photograph, which could happen if she refused to pay and the blackmailer was sufficiently fool-
hardy to send me that picture and tell her he was going
to. I didn't want her to know, and I didn't want her to
get into any trouble on account of it."

He put the letter opener down and said: "I decided
I had to know who was doing the blackmailing, and I
had no idea how to go about getting that information.
I was pretty sure she would get in touch with this man,
and I couldn't follow her, nor would I attempt to. I didn't
want anyone else to either and yet I had no choice. I
picked up a directory and I went to Mr. Epps simply

because, as you say, his office was just around the corner."

"He followed her starting yesterday morning?" Murdock asked.

Jerome nodded. "And he telephoned me last night, as you suspected. I drove there to meet him and when I arrived Epps said she had gone. I asked Epps if he knew who she had visited. He said he thought it was the second-floor apartment. Apparently he had checked the mailbox, because he said he thought it was occupied by Ralph Stacy, a reporter on the *Courier*. I got into my car and drove off."

"Leaving Epps there?"

"Yes."

Murdock thought it over, knowing somehow that this was all the explanation he was going to get out of Jerome. It made, he decided, a fairly straightforward and convincing story; the trouble was it did not have to be the truth, particularly the denouement.

He understood Jerome's motives for hiring Epps, but he also knew that men Jerome's age who had young wives with the looks and figure of Vivian Jerome were often more than a little jealous of such wives. He remembered one instance of a man somewhat older than Jerome, as well as richer, who went about with a gun in his pocket, threatening the young men who so much as disappeared from a dance floor with his wife and, in one case, going so far as to shoot the offender in the leg in a minor scandal that never reached the newspapers.

Jerome knew where his wife had gone. Jerome could have left as he now stated. It seemed more probable that he had taken the next step on his own and gone to see Stacy last night. But since this was a matter of conjecture and, at the moment, outside his province, Murdock stood up.

"I suppose it's too much to ask that you keep all this

confidential," Jerome said, watching him closely but with no outward display of animosity.

"If you mean will there be any publicity from me," Murdock said, "the answer is no. You can forget about the picture as far as I'm concerned. The police won't have to know about it, but if they ask me about you and Epps I'll have to tell them. They already know Epps was hanging around Stacy's last night, so you can figure it out from there."

Jerome stood up, dispirited but not defeated. He said he appreciated what Murdock had done about the photograph, and that he assumed nothing of the present conversation would be repeated to his wife.

14

IT WAS habit that took Murdock back to the *Courier* shortly after four o'clock. The Studio was empty at the moment, but there was a message on his desk asking him to call Mrs. Stacy along with a notation of her telephone number. He repeated it to the *Courier* operator without bothering to take off his hat or coat.

"Hello, Mr. Murdock," Elinor Stacy said. "I know you're busy, but I've been thinking about those films I gave you all day. Were you able to find out anything?"

"Quite a lot."

"And were they—well, what you were afraid they might be?"

"It looks that way," Murdock said.

There was a pause and what she said next indicated she had used it to get nerve enough to make the request.

"I'd like to know the truth," she said. "I don't suppose you want to discuss it over the telephone, but I'll be here a few minutes longer and I wonder if you could stop by."

Murdock glanced up as Bush came in, looking very proud and smoking one of his own cigars. Murdock eyed him glumly, tired of talking or even thinking about Stacy, but aware too that Elinor Stacy had a right to know what he'd done with the films she had given him.

"I'd be glad to, Mrs. Stacy," he said. "I'll be there in ten minutes."

A considerable change had been made in the Stacy apartment since morning. The contents of the desk had been neatly stacked in a cardboard carton, and another, larger carton was filled with books. The woodwork looked spotless and when he spoke of this Elinor Stacy summoned a small smile to show she was pleased at what he said.

"There was a lot to be done," she said, "but I think the worst of it is over."

She brushed her brown hair away from her brow with the back of her hand and he could see that lines of weariness had begun to work on her plain-looking face. For all of this, there was a twinkle in her light-blue eyes as he glanced up from an inspection of an old-fashioned market basket which had been loaded with bottles.

"I could give you a drink," she said. "I'm sure you deserve it. . . . I decided there was no point in leaving those here," she said. "Now, when I need a nightcap sometime I'll have it."

Murdock glanced again at the bottles of Scotch and bourbon and gin and vermouth, and though he could have used a drink he did not want to take the trouble of fixing it.

"You're not going to stay here, then?" he said.

"Oh, no. I—I couldn't. Not now. The place I have will do until I can find something better." She paused, tilting her head. "I've about finished here and if you wouldn't mind carrying that basket we could walk to the other apartment—it isn't far—and talk on the way. I'll get my coat."

She said nothing more until they were down on the sidewalk. Then, taking his free arm lightly, she looked up at him.

"I'm not going to ask you *how* you know," she said. "I just want to be sure that you are sure. Had Ralph been blackmailing people, Mr. Murdock?"

"Yes," said Murdock. "He had. And for quite a while."

He heard her sigh. She walked three steps, her gaze fixed straight ahead now and her voice quiet.

"Then I guess it's all right for me to tell you that I lied a little this morning."

"Oh?"

"You asked me if I suspected Ralph might be doing such a thing and I said no, and that was wrong. I was never sure, but I did *suspect* him."

"But he never admitted it?"

"I never accused him. But from certain telephone calls he would get and the things he said—well, it seemed odd to me. Once or twice I asked him and he shut me up by saying it was business. Sometimes he seemed afraid, I think. I do know that he was making more money than he ever let me know about. I had a pretty good idea what salary he made, and that wasn't enough to buy a car like he had and go to the places he did night after night.

"He certainly didn't spend it on me or the apartment," she said. "You've seen the furniture. You could buy the whole lot for the price of the car. Sometimes when he was drunk he'd hint that he didn't have to worry about money and one day—this was nearly three years ago— he took me to the bank and hired a safe-deposit box. I don't know why he wanted my name on the card, but he did. I never heard any more about it. He kept the keys and I never even saw the inside of that box."

"Have you found out yet about his bank account?"

"My lawyer did. He said there was twelve hundred and some dollars in Ralph's account."

"Did you tell the lawyer about the safe-deposit box?"

"Yes, but it was nearly three o'clock when he phoned me. He said he would try to find out about it tomorrow and asked if I knew where the keys were. I told him I hadn't found them," she said and glanced up again. "Could you tell me if the police have them?"

Murdock, remembering the things which had been taken from Stacy's pockets, said he did not think the police had found any safe-deposit keys. She was silent for a few more steps as they turned the corner.

"Suppose I don't find them?" she asked finally.

Murdock said he wasn't sure, but that since she could prove the box was in her name he thought the bank would chisel it open and she'd have to pay for it. "The tax men will probably want to have a look at that box, too," he said. "Your lawyer will know about that."

"Well," she said, digressing again, "I'm glad I gave you the films. I'm also glad I don't know anything about them because now if the police ask me I can tell the truth. Will you"—her hand touched his arm again—"have to tell them where you got them?"

"Probably," Murdock said, adding under his breath: "If I turn them over at all."

They turned into her apartment-house foyer, and now, approaching the elevator, Murdock remembered something else.

"You work for Mr. Jerome, don't you?"

"Why, yes, I do," she said with some surprise.

"What kind of a man is he?"

"Oh, very much of a gentleman. He's very considerate."

"How did you happen to get the job? Did he advertise or—?"

"No." She hesitated again. "As a matter of fact I got

it through Ralph in a way. He knew I was looking for something part-time and one day he said why didn't I go see Mr. Jerome. He'd heard that there might be something in his office."

"Well," Murdock thought as they stepped out of the elevator, "that fits anyway."

He followed her to her door and as she fumbled for her key he said: "Did you know Mrs. Jerome came to see Ralph last night?"

"Mrs. Jerome?" she said. "Why would she—?"

That was as far as she got, and the thought, whatever it was, remained unsaid. For she had opened the door and had started into the living-room, and now she gasped aloud and stopped so suddenly Murdock ran into her.

He saw why an instant later as Elinor Stacy took another step and then stopped again to look about in consternation.

One glance was enough to tell Murdock that the room had been thoroughly searched by someone who had not bothered to disguise the fact. The studio couch had been pulled away from the wall, the pillows tumbled to the floor, and the mattress rolled back at one end. The thin scatter rugs had been tossed in a heap; the drawers of the table desk stood open.

He did not follow her into the bedroom but put the basket down and waited, puzzled before a semblance of an answer occurred to him, hearing the woman opening and closing drawers in the adjoining room to the accompaniment of small cries of exasperation and dismay. After a minute or so of this she came back to the living-room, hands fluttering and her eyes wide.

"Well!" she said explosively. "This is a fine thing."

"Is anything missing?" Murdock asked.

"Missing?" The idea seemed to sober her. "Why, no. Not that I know of. There's nothing here for anyone anyway. I have no money or jewelry. Why should—"

"What about films?"

"Films?"

"Sit down a minute, Mrs. Stacy."

Murdock watched her roll the couch mattress in place and put the pillows back. When she sat down and looked up at him his thoughts centered on the two men who had come to Stacy's place the night before to search the darkroom. They had apparently taken all the negatives in sight, but possibly not the right ones. The negatives that Stacy had hidden elsewhere were now in the envelope in his inside pocket, and this seemed the only possible explanation for what had happened. Now, putting his thoughts into words, he saw that she understood what he had in mind.

"You mean that the men who came last night didn't get what they wanted," she said. "They knew there must be others and they came here to look for them."

"Somebody must have," Murdock said. "Why else should anyone come here?"

She looked right at him. "Believe me, Mr. Murdock, the only films I know about are the ones I gave you this morning."

"But you and I are the only ones who know that. Somebody is apparently looking for a special negative. It wasn't at the other apartment—or so he thinks—so maybe it was here."

"Yes," she said. "I see."

For a moment then the little room was quiet. Murdock stood where he was, hands thrust into his coat pockets and his dark gaze disturbed as his mind went on to one more possibility.

"Did your husband spend much time with Nancy Larkin?"

She blinked at him and then her mouth tightened, as though this was a subject she would rather not discuss.

"I suppose he did," she said woodenly. "He was out to all hours."

"What I'm getting at is this," Murdock said. "Suppose he had a few special negatives, not the ones you found this morning but others. Couldn't he have left them at her place, figuring that if things got tough no one would ever think of looking there?"

"Yes, I suppose he could," she said. "It would be just like him."

"I think I'd better check and see," Murdock said. "You'd better keep your door locked when you're here," he added, "but I doubt if you'll be bothered again."

He left then and the slow descent of the elevator bothered him. When he reached the street his stride was hard-heeled and quick. He did not notice the two girls playing jacks on the sidewalk. When he turned the corner the half-dozen youngsters playing their own version of baseball in the street were nothing more than noisy animated figures. For the trouble was still kicking around in his mind and the progression bothered him.

Stacy's place had been searched. His wife's place had been searched. Nancy Larkin might be next to anyone who happened to know of her affair with Stacy.

The entryway of Nancy Larkin's apartment looked even more discouraging in daylight than it had the night before. The strollers and the baby carriage were still there cluttering the foyer, and the food smells had changed very little from the night before as he went hurriedly along the second-floor hall.

He saw the key in the door as he started to knock. The sight of this made him pause and suddenly he felt an odd stirring inside him that was apprehensive and uncertain. Shaking it off, a little impatient with himself now, he knocked, knocked again when there was no answer. When he put his hand on the knob he did not have to touch the key because the latch had not clicked into place.

"Hello," he said, standing just inside the room with his hand still on the knob. "Anyone home?"

He saw then, as the silence of the room came back at him, that someone had been busy. The couch looked messy. The overdressed doll lay face-down on the floor alongside one of the pillows. The chest that Bacon had looked through the night before stood with its drawers partly open, and now, the tension beginning to pull at his nerve ends, he glanced again at the key in the door.

It was this that bothered him most, though he did not know why, and he left it where it was when he closed the door. Ahead and partly visible through the open door was a cubby that seemed to be a kitchenette. There was one other door opening from this room and he started for it, aware an instant later that it gave on a tiny hall. Directly ahead was the bedroom and, on his left, an open door leading to an unlighted bathroom.

Murdock did not enter the bedroom, nor the bath. For just then he heard this sound, faint but unmistakable and, to him, loud, urgent, and appalling. He wheeled instantly, the back of his neck suddenly cold. This brought him face to face with a closed door and he reached for the knob without hesitation, yanking it toward him.

He knew first that this was a closet, a deep and roomy cubicle, thick with gloom. On the pole stretched across it hung a coat and some dresses. Underneath them and partly obscured was a humplike object that did not belong there.

He noticed the patch of white first and it was so dark he could not tell what it was until he knelt down. Then, his heart turning swiftly over, he knew that what he saw was part of a thigh, exposed now by a hiked-up skirt.

In that interminable, horrified instant he could see

nothing more, and he had to reach forward, groping now, to know that a coat had been pulled upward to cover Nancy Larkin's head and shoulders. It was then, as he froze there, that he heard again the faint sound of moaning.

15

THE NEXT few seconds as he worked frantically in that gloomy closet had no reality for Murdock. His movements were automatic and came without conscious thought as he got his hands on the girl's shoulders, pulling her to a sitting position and easing her limp form out where he could get it in his arms. He knew then that she still wore the coat which had covered her and it trailed along the floor as he came erect and carried Nancy Larkin quickly to the couch.

He got one of the pillows under her blond head and pulled her skirt down and felt her hands. The moaning had stopped, and now, seeing her stir, he glanced up to find her eyes wide open and watching him.

"Hello," she said weakly, like a child who has just awakened from a sound sleep. "What happened?"

Murdock let his breath out slowly. He still held her hand and he found his own was trembling as the tension slid from his body and reaction set in.

"Take it easy, Nancy," he said huskily. "Be a good girl and stay right there. . . . Is there any whisky or brandy in the place?"

"There's a bottle of whisky," she whispered. "In the cabinet over the sink."

Murdock straightened and slid out of his coat. He snapped the light on in the kitchenette and found the bottle of bourbon without difficulty. He located the glasses and put one on the drainboard; then he reached for another. He poured out an inch of whisky, added the same amount of water. Into the second glass he put not quite so much whisky and no water. When he had tossed down his first drink of the day he carried the other glass in to the girl.

She had pushed up to a semi-sitting position, her weight supported on one stiff arm. The lipstick on her wide, mobile mouth and the touch of eye-shadow contrasted sharply with the temporary pallor of her skin, but her dark-blue eyes were clear as she looked up at him and accepted her glass.

She coughed when she took her first swallow and he grinned at her. "Take it slow," he said. "Sip it. Now another one and then we'll have a look at your head. Does it hurt?"

"A little. It sort of aches."

"You don't know who hit you?"

"No."

"Well, how did it happen? What did you do?"

She finished the rest of her drink and put the glass aside.

"I'd been out and I unlocked the door and started to open it." She lifted her hands an inch or two and let them drop. "That's all I remember. I don't remember coming inside or anything."

Murdock believed her because he knew that, when a person is knocked unconscious, he not only can't remember what happened to him but, in many cases, what happened immediately before that. Someone, it seemed, had been searching the place when she had started to unlock the door. Someone standing behind the opening panel had reached out to slug her before she could turn.

"Where was I?" she said, still regarding him openly. "Where did you find me?"

He told her. He said whoever hit her had carried her into the closet and pulled her coat over her head.

"Do you want to take it off?" he asked. He helped her with it and when she sat down on the edge of the couch he took her head gently in his hands as he stood in front of her. "Where does it hurt?" he asked. "Let's see."

She said she thought it hurt most near the back and dutifully lowered her head, forehead touching his coat front, legs clamped together and her hands on her skirted knees. He parted the hair, noting as he did so that the roots were the same shade of blondness, and now he saw the swelling just below the crown, an abraded spot with very little blood.

"Come on."

He took her by the hand and she walked with him to the bathroom. She leaned over the bowl when he told her to and stood there as unprotesting as a child while he found a clean washcloth and soaked the drying blood from the abrasion. He found a tiny bottle of Metaphen in the medicine cabinet and lightly coated the wound.

"Okay. . . . You're lucky it doesn't show," he said, while in the disturbed depths of his mind came the added thought that she might be lucky to be alive, that perhaps the best break of all had come from the fact that she had not seen the intruder.

He led her back to the couch and when she sat down he pulled a chair close to her.

"All right," he said.

She smiled at him but there was nothing coy about it. Her eyes said she liked him, and the whisky had done its work nobly, putting the color back in her cheeks and her emotions at ease.

"All right what?" she parried.

"Who would want to be searching this place, and for what?"

"I don't know. Honest, Mr. Murdock."

"You haven't got any hidden wealth around the place?"

"Nor anywhere else," she said. "I've got a savings account with a few hundred in it period."

Murdock reached for his cigarettes, the somber set of his angular face reflecting thoughts that had bogged down in discouragement. Why, he silently asked himself, was he horsing around with this business anyway? Because T. A. MacGrath had asked him to? Because of some curiosity of his own? Because of any obligation he felt to Stacy?

The answer to this was, he knew, no. He had done as MacGrath had asked to the best of his ability, and in all honesty he realized that he had no proper answers and actually knew very little more than he had before he started out that morning. Now, as he gave the girl a light and took one himself, it occurred to him that not only had he gone as far as he could with what he had to work with, but that somehow he had no desire to pursue the matter.

He had heard a lot of stories, some of which he believed and some of which he was not so sure of. People involved in murder cases lied when it suited them and when they thought they could get away with it, a theorem which applied not only to the killer. The way to break down the lies was to confront those involved with facts which were contrary and indisputable, and this was a job better done by the police.

Suddenly, out of the confusion of his mind, a resolution came to him. He was here and he had some questions he wanted to ask, but after that, the hell with it. He could tell Bacon what he knew and let the Lieutenant take it from there.

"Did Ralph spend much time here?" he asked.

The abruptness of the question seemed to startle her and her reply was faltering. "Well—yes, in a way."

"Did he ever speak to you about films, or negatives?
. . . Did he ever ask to leave anything with you?" he
pressed when she shook her head. "Like an envelope or
papers—"

"No," she said, interrupting. "The only thing he ever
left was whisky. He wanted to be sure there was always
some here."

"He always seemed to have plenty of money, didn't
he?"

"He seemed to."

"Did he ever boast about it or tell you how much he
made? Anything like that?"

"Not exactly. But"—she bunched her brows in a small
frown—"once when it was pretty late and he'd been
drinking a lot I said he ought to watch out or he'd lose
his job. I didn't really think that. I was only kidding."

"And what did he say?"

"He said the job didn't worry him any, that there were
other ways to make money if you knew your way around."

"He didn't say how?" Murdock asked hopefully.

"He said he had angles."

Murdock stood up, walked away from the chair, and
came back, his thoughts digressing swiftly now that he
had his answer. Not meaning to, he remembered Jack
Frost and the telephone call that had led him to Martin
Epps.

"You knew Stacy's wife was going to divorce him," he
said. "Did he ever say anything to you about leaving
town?"

"No, but"—her chin came up—"I would have gone with
him if he'd asked me to."

"I guess you didn't care any more about Frost," Murdock said, his tone crowding her intentionally. "He got
you your job when you needed one and tried to make
a singer out of you. You know why, don't you? Because

he was in love with you. Which was fine with you—until Stacy came along."

"But I didn't know it at first," she said, her eyes starting to glisten. "That Jack was in love with me, I mean. Nobody could have been kinder. He was sweet and considerate and—"

"Until last night," Murdock said.

"He didn't kill Ralph," she said hotly.

"You thought he was going to. You were so scared—"

"Of course I was scared. I knew Jack wouldn't do anything like that if he was sober and—well, I had to try to stop him. I didn't want anything to happen to Ralph, or to Jack either."

The tears were on her cheeks now and she might have said more had it not been for the knock that came to interrupt her. The unexpectedness of the sound startled her and as she glanced round the lock clicked and the door swung open.

Jack Frost stepped into the room, the key in his hand. He stood there a moment, tall and thin and threatening, his long face truculent and his eyes suspicious as they focused on Murdock and the girl.

"What's the idea of leaving the key in the lock?" he said. "You want to watch that or one of these days some thug will walk in on you." He moved up, his glance taking in the empty glass before he noticed the tears on the girl's face.

"You've been crying," he said. "Why? What's wrong?" He glared at Murdock. "What've you been doing to her?"

"It's not Mr. Murdock, Jack," she said quickly. "It's not his fault."

She was on her feet now as Frost stepped close. Then, as though she had struggled too long to keep her feelings in check, the wall of her reserve cracked wide and all the pent-up emotion spilled through. With a sob she could not stifle, she leaned against him, arms hanging limply, her blond head on his cheek.

"Oh, why did it have to happen?" she asked in muffled tones. "It's all my fault and—"

Frost cut her off as his arms went quickly about her. "Now, now," he said thickly. "Don't cry, baby. It'll be all right."

Murdock put on his coat and hat. By the time he got to the door the girl's sobs had quieted and Frost was saying: "That's the girl," and patting her shoulder. As he started along the hall it occurred to Murdock that, with Stacy out of the way, Frost might get his girl back after all.

It was after five when Kent Murdock arrived at his apartment, and what he did then was impulsive and, in some ways, not very smart. The nagging confusion in his mind was perhaps chiefly responsible for his act, but at the time he was physically exhausted and thoroughly disgusted with himself. He did not know who had killed Stacy, and as he considered most of those involved it surprised him to discover that he was sympathetic with most of them.

He liked Frost and Nancy Larkin and, in her quiet way, Elinor Stacy. He had been impressed by Randolph Jerome; he was more than a little taken with his wife, Vivian, and it seemed now that all he wanted to do was forget the whole thing, to stop pestering people, to leave well enough alone. Without realizing it and with no conscious effort on his part, the focal point of his dissatisfaction became the films he had in his pocket. For it was these negatives, unethically taken, collected, and exploited, that were the cause of his mental sickness. Because of them he had been on the go constantly since that morning. His accomplishments, as he saw them, added up to zero, and now, as this new idea came to him, he embraced it with enthusiasm.

There were some folded newspapers in the copper bucket beside the fireplace, and when he had removed the screen he tore one up and wadded it into several loose balls. As soon as he had touched a match to one of these he took out the envelope and emptied the remaining negatives and contact prints into his palm.

He tossed the envelope onto the spreading flames and when that caught he began to pitch the negatives after it, taking two or three at a time, watching them burst into flame and boil and bubble as the acrid smoke was sucked up the flue. It was all over in another minute and now, feeling immeasurably better, he went over to the telephone and dialed the *Courier's* number. When he had been connected with MacGrath he said:

"You can quit worrying about Stacy. And maybe you'd better soft-pedal the reward."

"What's the rest of it?" MacGrath asked quietly.

"He had some negatives. Pictures he'd taken here and there and kept to himself. He'd been tagging people for years."

There was a long silence, broken only by the remote sound of the managing editor's breathing. When he spoke again his voice sounded tired.

"All right," he said. "I'll take your word for that and I'm not interested in details. But I've got a question. He could still have been killed for something recent, couldn't he? Something he might have been doing for us without our knowing about it?"

"Sure," Murdock said. "But don't ask me what. You know about the two hoodlums who cleaned out his darkroom last night. They searched Mrs. Stacy's place this afternoon. Beyond that I'm not even going to guess for you."

MacGrath muttered something and hung up. Murdock racked his own instrument and it was then that he heard the click of a door behind him. When he turned to glance round he saw the two men watching him from the doorway.

He had not heard them open the door, nor did he know how much of the conversation they had heard. He did see the larger of the two putting something in his trousers pocket, apparently the keys he had used to gain entrance. They watched him steadily, two men in form-fitting blue coats, one a heavily built husky with a swart complexion and thick brows that met over the bridge of his nose. His companion was more slender. Younger too, with blond hair that needed a trim, and dark glasses.

Murdock seemed to know who they were, for he remembered what Mrs. Stacy had said about the bare-headed blond man who had struck her down the night before. The sight of them now infuriated him and without saying a word he turned back to the telephone and started to dial.

"Put it back, Mac," a voice said. "Or do I pop it out of your hand?"

Something about the flat, unaccented tone stopped Murdock with his finger still in the dial and his number incomplete. When he glanced over his shoulder the blond man had a gun in his hand and a mean grin on his face.

Murdock replaced the telephone. He rose and walked slowly toward them, one eye on the automatic. "What do you want?"

"We want to look around," the dark man said, pushing back a porkpie hat that looked silly on his balding head. "We thought we'd have to do it all by ourselves."

"You can help us look," his companion said.

"For what?"

"Films. You're a photographer, aren't you?"

"So you didn't get what you wanted last night?"

"No."

"What did you have to slug the woman for?" A casual question, asked in the hope of confirming Murdock's suspicion.

"Because she started to—" The blond youth stopped when his companion jabbed him with an elbow.

"Shut up! . . . The films, sucker," the big man said to Murdock. "Which way?"

"Turn around, Mac," the blond said and gestured with the gun.

Murdock obeyed. He could feel the man move up behind him, and presently the muzzle of the gun jabbed him below his right shoulder. The blond said: "March!" and Murdock took a slow deliberate step. When he hesitated again the gun jabbed him in the same spot. He took another step, felt the following jab, and now there was a regular rhythm to his slow progress toward the open door next to the kitchen.

He could see his apron hanging on the back of that door, the bench and part of the sink beyond. The thought of what might happen kept the fury churning inside him, but, unlike the fit of temper he had displayed at Phil Avery's place, this feeling was cold and calculating and relentless.

For in his darkroom files he had hundreds of negatives which had been accumulated over the years. To him many of them seemed priceless and none could be replaced. These two—hired by someone who at the moment seemed unimportant—had come for a particular negative. Of this he felt certain, just as he was sure that they would never take the time to go through his files and try to find the one they wanted. What they would do was take everything they could find. Those negatives would be gone forever.

With but three or four steps to go, the idea came to him and he acted on it because he had no more time.

He knew it would be silly to try to turn. Even if he made it without getting shot he had no thought that he could take the two of them. To get knocked out would be equally bad, so he based his plan on the only weakness he could find: the blond youth's arrogant overconfidence.

He took his next step, hesitating until the gun jabbed him. He took the one after that. Then, when he should have hesitated, he stooped suddenly and the gun, aimed at his shoulder as before, shot over it and past it.

Reaching up, Murdock grabbed the wrist, pulling hard and at the same time backing up a half-step to get more leverage. In a continuation of the same movement his left hand joined his right. He heaved, getting his shoulder into it and twisting the arm as he applied his pressure.

Perhaps a second had passed. It took approximately the same time to complete the operation, which he had learned the hard way in Italy. The blond, off balance from the beginning, sailed over Murdock's shoulder and crashed downward, the back of his neck, his buttocks, and his heels shaking the floor in that order. Simultaneously Murdock slipped the automatic from limp fingers.

The swart man, as surprised as his companion, never got into the act. He had watched the performance with open-mouthed amazement and by the time he could react his only concern was the gun which now covered him.

"Okay, Porkpie," Murdock said. "Drag him out of there."

The blond was moaning but motionless. He lay half in and half out of the darkroom, and when the big man got his hands under his companion's armpits and started to lift, the blond yelped.

"No," he said. "Jesus, my back's broken!"

"Pick him up," Murdock said. "That's right. Now bring him over here and prop him up on the couch. . . . Come on, Blondie," he said. "You're not hurt."

When the two were on the divan, Murdock backed to the telephone. With a warning to the big man to keep his hands in sight, he dialed Police Headquarters and after a few seconds Bacon's voice came on the wire.

"I've got those two guys who got tough with Mrs. Stacy last night," Murdock said.

"You've got what?" said Bacon. "Where?"

"Here, at my place. You'd better bring someone with you."

He hung up and looked at his captives. The blond was grunting in a labored sort of way and his companion sat there sullenly in his silly-looking hat. Murdock grinned at them. He was not sure what all this proved, but he felt a lot better.

16

LIEUTENANT BACON arrived ten minutes later with Sergeant Keogh and two plainclothesmen. When Murdock opened the door Bacon glanced at the automatic and put out his hand. Murdock handed over the gun and Bacon examined it. Slipping it into the pocket of his straight-hanging coat, he advanced toward the two men on the divan, a stiff-backed, forbidding figure with a tight, unsmiling face and hard gray eyes. After a second of silent and contemptuous appraisal he glanced at Murdock.

"Did you fan 'em?" he said.

"No."

"Stand up!" Bacon said. "Keogh!"

The blond protested. He cringed. He said he couldn't stand up. When he said his back was broken, Keogh simply reached for him and stood him on his feet in spite of the anguished cry that accompanied the move. After that the two of them were still while Keogh searched them, the blond a little hunched but apparently not mortally injured.

There was no other gun, nor any word spoken until Keogh stepped back and said: "Clean."

"You still working for Joe Calenda, Albert?" Bacon said to the big man.

No answer.

"Who's your pal?"

No answer.

Bacon turned to Murdock. "Who had the gun?"

"Blondie."

"What happened?"

Murdock told him and Bacon chewed on the information. "These could be the two that called at Stacy's last night," he said. "That guy that was walking the dog said one of 'em was a blond."

Murdock said he was sure they were the same two. "I asked them why they slugged Mrs. Stacy," he said, "and Blondie started to tell me before Porkpie shut him up."

Bacon turned to his two detectives. "You know either of these hoods?"

"The fat guy," said one of them, "used to be an odd-job boy for Joe Calenda."

"You still on Joe's payroll?" Bacon said to the big man.

"You're wastin' your breath," the man said.

"Am I?"

"We'll talk to you—maybe—after we talk to a mouthpiece."

"That may be quite a while," Bacon said mildly.

"Nuts," Blondie said, finding his voice. "Joe'll spring us—"

His companion eyed him scornfully. "Will you stay shut?" he snapped.

Bacon almost smiled as he watched the two. "Joe will have to find you first." He glanced at Murdock, hands clasped behind his back and under his coattails. "Stacy did a pretty good job on Calenda awhile back," he said thoughtfully.

Murdock remembered his own thoughts the night before when the two shots had been fired at Stacy's car. At that time he had wondered if the motive behind the attempt was the same one that had prompted a similar attempt six months earlier.

Locally, the key figure in the investigation was Joe Calenda, who over the years had set up an interlocking system of rackets and graft that had given him a stranglehold on the city's produce markets. He owned a warehousing business which had been set up as a corporation in his wife's name. His trucking business was ostensibly owned by his two sons-in-law, while at the same time he acted as president of the local which ran things, though Murdock could not remember just which union this was. Through strategically placed assistants he exacted tribute all along the line, his own position so secure that he had been named to a place on the State Industrial Commission.

All that had changed since Stacy came into the picture. When the story broke the Governor bounced Calenda from the Commission, and the national union ousted him as president and put in a trustee to run the local. He had been convicted of extortion and was free on bail pending an appeal; he still had to face an indictment of several counts of perjury, and the income-tax people were now ready to pounce.

All this Murdock knew, but he still could not understand why Calenda was looking for Stacy's negatives at this late date. Neither, it seemed, could Bacon.

"You got any ideas on this?" he asked.

"I've got some ideas," Murdock said, "but not about Calenda."

Bacon thought it over and then made up his mind.

"Take 'em out to Mattappan," he said to Keogh and the two detectives. "We've got 'em any time we want on larceny and assault with a dangerous weapon for what happened last night." He regarded Murdock narrowly. "Will you keep this out of the paper?"

"Sure." Murdock grinned. "I'm on detached duty for a while."

"We can book them on disorderly conduct or vagrancy if we have to," Bacon said to Keogh, "but maybe we won't have to until Joe finds out where they are. That ought to take a couple of days and maybe by that time they'll change their minds about talking." He took the automatic and gave it to Keogh. "When you get out there you can find out if the punk is carrying a permit. Tell the captain I'll call him."

He punctuated the order with a jerk of his head and the procession got under way. When the door had closed and the room was again quiet, Bacon pushed his hat back and sat down on the arm of a chair.

"Let's you and me have a little chat," he said.

Murdock had an idea of what was coming. Bacon had finished with the routine of police work for the moment, but he was far too shrewd an officer to accept the incident at face value. There were things that had to be explained and now Murdock sat down and prepared himself mentally for what was to come.

"Check me if I'm wrong," Bacon said. "Joe Calenda sends two guys to Stacy's place to get a film, or a negative, or whatever you want to call it. They clean out Stacy's files, but apparently they don't get what they want, otherwise they wouldn't have come here."

"They may also have gone to Mrs. Stacy's place this

afternoon," Murdock said and went on to tell what had happened there and at Nancy Larkin's apartment.

Bacon digested these facts slowly because they were new to him and required some thought. For perhaps five seconds he sat unmoving, his gray gaze fixed at some point outside the room's windows. When he was ready he said:

"All right. So they finally came here. Why?"

"They probably found out I was at Stacy's last night," Murdock said. "They may have figured Stacy gave me the negative, or that I knew something about it."

"Did he?"

"What?"

"Give you the negative."

"No."

Bacon took a breath and struggled with his patience. "That's not good enough. You can do better than that," he said. "Stacy didn't give you anything, but some films are missing and you know something about them."

"Yes."

"Well," said Bacon, a snap in his tone, "what the hell're you stalling around for?"

"This is going to take a while." Murdock glanced at his strap watch. "Are you going to eat in town tonight?"

"Sure. You think I got time to—"

"Well, will you have dinner with me? We can eat and I can tell you what I know at the same time."

Bacon considered the proposition and accepted. "Okay," he said. "We eat dinner, but I pay for my own."

Murdock grinned at him, understanding how it was with Bacon and respecting his views. He said all right. "But when we get wherever we're going," he said, "I'm going to have a drink, and you won't because people'll see you and you'll consider yourself on duty. So you'd better have one here before you go."

Lieutenant Bacon had a very nice smile when he gave

it a chance and now he let himself go. "You've sold me, kid," he said. "Make it whisky—if you've got any *good* whisky—with a little water, and never mind the ice."

17

ON THE ride downtown Murdock and Bacon argued a bit about where they could eat. Not knowing how the lieutenant felt about it, Murdock said he knew a little place where they could get a good lobster or a tender steak. Bacon refused.

"To hell with these little places," he said. "When I eat with a newspaperman I don't want it to look like I'm covering up. We'll eat out in the open."

Murdock grinned. "You're awfully damned sensitive about it."

Bacon merely growled.

"Then how about Locke-Ober?"

"Too expensive." Bacon growled again. "Why do we have to be so fancy? What's wrong with Parsons'?"

Murdock said Parsons' was fine with him, so they went to this place that had very little style and no atmosphere. The tables were white-topped, the walls held no pictures, and the floor was tiled in an old-fashioned way. The condiments, ketchup, mustard, and relish, were always on the table, the silverware was plated and worn, and there was light enough to read a menu without having to peer at it. There was a bar, but it was strictly a working bar and there were no stools to induce a customer to linger. But the service, handled by elderly men and women, was excellent though unhurried and there was no better seafood served in the city.

Murdock did not bother with the menu. He ordered Scotch-on-rocks and asked if Bacon liked lobster.

"Yes," said Bacon, "and I can't get it at home because my wife says every time she cooks it, it smells up the house, though I don't know why the hell it should."

"A pound-and-a-quarter one for me," Murdock told the waiter. "And a pound-and-three-quarter one for my father. . . . Salad?"

Bacon sighed. "Yeah, I guess so," he said with some reluctance. "It's supposed to be good for you. . . . A small one," he said to the waiter. "And French fries, and coffee with the dinner for me, and bring separate checks."

He leaned back and watched Murdock sip his drink. "It's going to take a few minutes for those lobsters," he said. "We could get started, couldn't we? What about those films?"

"Before I get into that," Murdock said, "who was the fellow in the picture I identified for you this morning?"

"What fellow?"

"The one that came to the office yesterday afternoon looking for Stacy. The one who witnessed the accident and wanted—"

"Oh, him." Bacon grunted softly. "Funny how things work out," he said. "That guy's not worth a damn to us because he had a good alibi for last night, but the F.B.I. were mighty pleased that we picked him up. . . . Remember that first batch of Commies that were convicted back in forty-nine or fifty?"

"Vaguely."

"Some of them went to prison like good boys, but some of 'em jumped the twenty-thousand bail. One they picked up later in Mexico or someplace, and some they never did get. . . . Well, this guy was one of them. Been working here for years and hiding out. Working as a counterman in a cafeteria—remember he had a white coat on? —and went out to look at the accident and got his picture

taken. Afraid to have it published, so he tried to reach
Stacy and missed. When he didn't see that picture in the
Courier he figured he was safe enough, so he was still
at the cafeteria when we picked him up this morning.
Right off we spotted his story as a phony, so the boys
kept after him and somebody got the idea of checking
with the F.B.I. and the minute we mentioned it he
cracked. . . . Now what about those films Stacy had—
but didn't give to you?"

The only negative and contact print that Murdock had
left were the ones he had put in his pocket that morning
showing the retired police captain and the two men, one
of whom was a convicted bookmaker. Now he put the
little print on the table and shoved it toward Bacon.

"You'd better get out your glasses," he said.

Bacon did so. He examined the print. When he was
satisfied he tossed the picture back on the table and put
away his glasses.

"What about it?" he said disgustedly. "That guy was
a thief, but he's no longer on the force." He started to
lean back again and then he stopped, his gaze suddenly
narrow. "That picture must have been taken a couple of
years ago. Where'd you get it?"

"I'll tell you in a minute," Murdock said, "but first tell
me what you do when you find out a cop is crooked."

Bacon's face twisted, not so much because he resented
the question as because he found the subject distasteful.
He was well aware that there are crooked policemen
just as there are crooked storekeepers and accountants,
but it was something he did not like to think about.

"It happens once in a while at all levels, doesn't it?"
Murdock pressed.

"Sure. A guy pounding a beat can be just as wrong
as a precinct captain. We don't get much of that in
Homicide, and I don't know what the hell you're drivin'
at, but what happens when a guy turns crooked depends

on a lot of things. It don't look good for the department and we don't like it to get out if we can help it because we get enough bad publicity from some of you newspaper guys as it is."

"You cover up for him."

"Until we can ease him out. But it ain't always easy and it can't always be done. If it gets bad enough— and it's seldom just one guy; he's generally got help— you eventually get a big stink like that one in New York, and then the thing blows wide open and every honest cop—which means most of them—has to take the rap. . . . Why?" he demanded, irritable now because he had been forced to discuss a matter he preferred to forget. "What's that got to do with—"

"I'll tell you," Murdock said, "but humor me, will you? Let me do it my way. . . . We don't have much trouble that way in my business and that's a pretty good testimonial to the integrity of the profession because the opportunity is always there. With a photographer there's always somebody who wants his picture in the paper or wants to keep it out, and plenty of them are willing to pay a little something for the favor. It's the same with reporters because they can slant a story in many ways and color facts—and sometimes they have to if that happens to be the policy of the publisher."

He finished his drink and said: "There are ways for a reporter to make a little extra on the side. A lot of them have little accounts and draw small checks for doing publicity for a promoter or a fighter or a politician. Those things are known and generally accepted, provided they are out in the open and there is no conflict. The newspaper business has never been overpaid and a legitimate sideline helps to keep a man satisfied. But now and then, just as in any business, we get a bad one. There was a fellow in Chicago a long time ago."

"I remember," Bacon said. "He got himself shot."

"Because he got himself in the middle. There was a big fuss in all the papers until they found out he had been playing with the mobs all along." He took a breath and said: "Well, Stacy was one of those and nobody on the paper suspected it."

"What?"

"Like the captain in that picture," Murdock said, "Ralph Stacy was a thief."

The arrival of the lobsters forestalled Bacon's immediate comment and, once started, he gave the food his full attention. Not until the plates had been taken away and he had his second cup of coffee did he resume his questioning.

"You're sure?" he said. "About Stacy, I mean?"

"I found it out today," Murdock said and then told his story briefly, explaining how Mrs. Stacy had given him the envelope containing negatives and prints and what he had done with them subsequently. He spoke of his calls on Phil Avery and Frank Deegan.

"It ties in," Bacon said. "Stacy must have tried to tap Calenda again and Joe sent those hoods snooping. What did you do with the rest of the negatives?"

"I burned them," Murdock said and set himself for the blast, which followed instantly.

"What?" said Bacon. "You what?" He examined Murdock with bright, incredulous eyes. "Why, Goddammit, those films were evidence. You deliberately destroyed them. You only checked on three or four. How about the others? . . ."

He had more to say on the subject, a lot more. Murdock let him go because he felt the attack was, from the lieutenant's viewpoint, justified. Not until Bacon ran out of words did Murdock offer a rebuttal.

"That envelope belonged to Mrs. Stacy," he said. "She gave it to me. She didn't have to. She didn't have to say anything about it, and neither did I. I could have burned

those negatives and said nothing." He hesitated to let
the logic of his words sink in and then he said: "I found
out a couple of other leads you may not know about.
Do you want to hear them?"

"Sure I want to hear them." Bacon began to manicure
a panetela, his neck still red but his irritation beginning
to dissipate. "It was a damn fool thing to do," he grum-
bled.

"Maybe." Murdock tipped one hand. "Maybe if you
went through all of the negatives you'd come up with a
clue that would help, but in the process you'd be scaring
a lot of innocent people half to death. So let's just say
I was wrong in burning them. You have my apologies,
but at the time I'd had all I wanted of Stacy, and his
chiseling, and all it stood for. . . . And anyway," he
said, his grin crooked, "I thought you were sold on the
triangle motive."

"It still could be that," Bacon said defensively, "and
don't think it couldn't. Now what about this other stuff
you know?"

"I found out who the woman in the camel's-hair coat
was."

Bacon leaned slowly forward, skeptical but impressed.
"You found out?" he asked. "Or you knew last night
and held out on us? . . . How do you know?" he demanded.

Murdock told him about the maroon Hillman and how
he had checked the owner.

"You knew about that Hillman last night," Bacon said
accusingly.

"I told you."

"Not that it was a maroon convertible."

"I forgot about it then."

Bacon blew smoke out with a gust of his breath. "I'll
give you one thing," he said. "When you want to use
it you've got a well-equipped forgettery."

"I'm telling you," Murdock argued, "I forgot it."

"Okay. So who was the dame?"

"Mrs. Randolph Jerome."

"Jerome." Bacon savored the word and found it familiar. "The society Jerome? An amateur yachtsman with a real-estate office? . . . Hmm," he said when Murdock nodded.

"Now what the hell," he added, wondering aloud, "would she want with Stacy?"

"Maybe he was trying to tap her about something," Murdock said, his mind made up that he would make no mention of the nude photograph. "There's something else," he said. "I think her husband had Martin Epps working on some job. . . . By the way, what did Epps have to offer?"

"One thing at a time," Bacon said. "What makes you think Epps was working for Jerome?"

"I saw him coming along the hall where Epps has his office," Murdock said and explained the circumstances.

Bacon peered at him. "Have you talked to Jerome?"

"Yes."

"I might have known it," Bacon said with a touch of asperity. He sighed and tried hard to keep the sarcasm from his manner, even though he didn't quite make it. "I guess you just had to talk to him before you could talk to me. . . . Well, what did he have to offer—if I'm not getting too personal."

Murdock let the sarcasm bounce off him. "You'd better ask him," he said.

"Don't think I won't," Bacon said. "But I want it from you too."

"Some of it was confidential," Murdock said.

"Now wait a minute." Bacon took the cigar from his mouth and pointed it. "Don't give me that guff about

newspapermen having the right to protect their pipe-
lines."

"It's stood up in court on occasion," Murdock said dog-
gedly.

"Not on murder cases."

"Before you bust an artery," Murdock said, "let me
tell you what I think. . . . I think Jerome was worried
about his wife," he said when Bacon made no reply. "I
think he hired Epps to find out who she was seeing and
Epps followed her to Stacy's last night. I think Epps went
to the drugstore to phone Jerome and I think Jerome
came down to see what it was all about. What happened
then I don't know and Jerome wouldn't tell me. You can
figure it out several different ways and one of them will
probably be right. . . . One thing more," he said before
Bacon could comment. "Did you know Mrs. Stacy
worked for Jerome part-time?"

"Sure," Bacon said. "I told you this morning I'd
checked on the guy she worked for."

"You didn't mention his name."

"Is it important?" Bacon came to attention again as he
nursed the new thought. "You think there's any monkey
business between Jerome and Mrs. Stacy?"

"No," Murdock said, "and when you get a look at
Vivian Jerome you'll know why. She's got looks, style, the
kind of figure—"

"Wait a minute," Bacon said dryly. "You're talking like
a boy. I'm not saying there's anything in the idea, but
a guy like you ought to know about lookers. They know
they're lookers and they never forget it even if they
wanted to because men keep reminding them of the fact."

He hesitated, smoking his panetela in small, tidy puffs
and enjoying each and every one of them as he expanded
his philosophy.

"The trouble with a looker," he said, "is that she gets
the idea all she has to do is *be* a looker. She spends all

her time looking beautiful, expecting things to drop in her lap with no effort on her part. It gets to be a habit. She works at just one thing: being beautiful. . . . A plain woman knows better. She has to work at her job whether she's a stenographer, housewife, or somebody's mistress, and she's willing to make the necessary sacrifices to get what she wants. She has to be four times better at any given thing than a looker to get by, and you know it."

He considered his oration and seemed pleased with it. More condescendingly he said: "I'm not even suggesting there was any affair between Jerome and Mrs. Stacy, but it's happened plenty of times before, brother. More lookers flock into the divorce courts than plain-looking women, and do you know why?"

"Because," said Murdock, grinning now, "the plain woman knows how to take care of her man."

"Go ahead and laugh," Bacon said, flushing slightly, "but I'm right and you know it."

"All right. You've got a sound theory. I don't know just how it fits this case, but maybe it does. So what about Epps? What did he say?"

"He says you're a liar."

"I thought he would."

"He says he wasn't there and you must have seen some-one else. We asked who he was working for and he said he didn't have to tell us, so we let it pass for the time being. Knowing what I know now, I'd have held him overnight and put some pressure on him, but as it was it looked smarter to give him plenty of rope and see where he led us. Hell, we can pick him up any time."

"Have you got a tail on him?"

"He'd spot a tail in a minute," Bacon said. "That's his business. We've got a stake-out at his apartment and office. That ought to do until I can check Jerome. . . . I don't know whether I should have a little talk with Joe Calenda or not," he said as his thoughts moved on.

"Probably wouldn't do much good," he said, answering himself. "We can put those two hoodlums away for sure if Mrs. Stacy can identify them. . . . You think they're the ones who searched her place this afternoon?"

"Who else would?"

"You think for those negatives, hunh?" He examined his cigar a moment and then gave Murdock a moment of narrow-eyed inspection. "And what are you going to do now?" he asked.

"Nothing."

"You're finished, hunh? You found out Stacy was a thief and now everything tastes lousy. You don't care much who killed him and the hell with it, is that the way it is?"

Murdock mumbled that it was something like that and Bacon said: "So I'm going to ask you something. Just give it a ripple before you say no."

The thing that was in Bacon's mind was not a spur-of-the-moment suggestion. He had been considering it with care, and his decision was based on his own personal knowledge of the photographer. He had known Murdock a long time. He respected him even when there was a difference of opinion and their objectives did not coincide. For Murdock's job was to provide newsworthy photographs for a big-city newspaper and he was hell-bent on doing just that when the opportunity presented itself. He had helped the police in the past on more than one occasion, sometimes because he knew co-operation would bring the photographs he wanted and sometimes because of some personal consideration. In this case he had an idea that Murdock was not concerned with photographs as such; he had an idea that Murdock would prefer to forget all about the case. He also knew that Murdock could give him more background on Stacy and his activities than anyone in the police department, so he decided to take a chance and ask a favor.

"This is off the record," he said. "I wouldn't want it to get around and you can tell me to go to hell if you like. I never asked you anything like this before, but there's always a first time. The point is—I could use some help. So far I think everybody involved is lying his head off and that's okay because it's something we expect. But you knew Stacy and you know about the negatives and maybe you can fill me in on some things later on if you'll stay with this another day or so."

Murdock eyed him with wonderment in that first instant. Only his own keen perception, and an understanding of the man which had been born of long association, kept him from laughing aloud because this was such a switch from the lieutenant's customary attitude. Usually Bacon was telling him to mind his own business—in an irascible but good-natured way—and stay out of his, Bacon's, hair. Now, considering his own respect and admiration for the man, he knew the effort it must have taken for Bacon to throw the book out the window and put his thoughts into words. The effect of all this on Murdock was immediate, and the smile that was reflected deep down in his eyes was understanding and a little proud.

"You're awfully damned afraid I might tell someone, aren't you?" he said. "Sure. I'll keep circulating for another day—not that it will do much good."

"You never can tell." Bacon's lips moved up at the corners. "With your kind of luck anything is possible."

Murdock called for the checks and suddenly, as though stimulated by the impetus of this new bargain with Bacon, he remembered something else.

"I found out this afternoon that Stacy had a safe-deposit box," he said. "Mrs. Stacy was a joint tenant, or whatever you call it. Maybe she—"

"Un-unh." Bacon shook his head. "We checked that. When my man was finding out about Stacy's checking-account he quizzed the manager of the safe-deposit department. Mrs. Stacy's signature is on the original card and that's all. To get into a box you have to sign. She never did. Unless Stacy told her, she couldn't even know what was in the box."

He leaned forward, lowering his voice. "And here's something you don't know. Stacy cleaned that box out yesterday morning. Came in with a briefcase, turned in the key, and closed out the box. What do you think was in it? More negatives? Cash?"

"Maybe both," Murdock said, his idea collapsing. "You figure it."

"There are two other banks in that neighborhood," Bacon said. "Stacy didn't rent a new box with either of them. We'll have to check all over town to be sure, but if you want my guess he was getting ready to blow town— with or without that blond Larkin dame. Maybe she knew it and maybe she didn't. My guess is that he was collecting what he could on any old negative he had that would stand the tap. I say he was getting ready to blow and someone cut him down."

He reached for his check and put on his glasses to inspect the total. He extracted an old wallet from some inner recess of the shiny suit and counted out the payment and tip.

"I'm glad you put me on to that Jerome thing," he said. "A dame like that, married to a rich society guy" —he smiled thinly—"especially when she's enough of a beauty to tip a guy like you over, and who has got a real soft spot and knows it—you take a dame like that and mix her up with a wrongie like Stacy and she'd fight to protect what she's got. . . . You want me to drop you by your office?"

Murdock said no. He said it was a nice night and he needed the exercise to shake the lobster down. He asked

Bacon if he enjoyed the dinner and the lieutenant said
it was excellent.

18

MURDOCK WAS right about the evening. A half-moon
which had risen somewhat earlier out of the Atlantic had
poked its face sufficiently skyward to clear the buildings
rimming the east side of the Common, its brilliance dim-
ming the stars as Murdock stared down Tremont Street.
Pedestrian traffic on the wide sidewalk was moderate
and composed chiefly of window-shoppers, with here and
there a strolling couple who found the evening pleasant.
Farther down, under lighted marquees, the movie houses
were doing a good business and Murdock was still a
block away from them when someone called his name.

He turned toward the curb and the one-way traffic
moving there. Parking was prohibited on this side of the
street, but he saw that a heavy black sedan had stopped
opposite him, its front door swinging open. The man who
got out was about six feet four inches tall and must
have weighed two hundred seventy pounds. The strollers
had to detour around him as he approached Murdock,
and, once past, they turned to examine him.

"Mr. Murdock?" he said, his voice thick but softly ca-
denced. "Mr. Calenda would like to speak to you."

By that time Murdock had noticed the lowered window in the car and now he saw the round face looking
out at him. When he was sure Calenda was alone he
walked over to the sedan.

"Is this coincidence, Joe?" he said. "Just happened to
be passing?"

"I followed you and Bacon from your place," Calenda

said. "We had to wait until you finished dinner." He opened the door. "All right, Lou," he said to the giant. "No use picking up a summons. Get in, Murdock. We can have a little talk while we ride."

"Any special place in mind?"

"Just around. Any place you say," Calenda said. "It won't take much of your time."

"Move over," Murdock said, and climbed in beside him.

The doors clicked shut and the sedan rolled sedately down the street, angling gradually to get into the right-hand traffic lane. The artificial brilliance of a theater marquee splashed light through the car's windows to give Murdock a glimpse of the plump, round-faced man beside him, dressed now in a dark suit and coat and a gray hat, a small man staring straight ahead as he slumped back on the seat cushions.

Remembering other times he had seen Joe Calenda, it occurred to Murdock that he did not look much like a man who had built up a tight little empire outside the law, a crumbling empire now but one that had been sustained by force, violence, and the constant fear of reprisal. Calenda did not look violent, nor did he talk that way; he looked more like a moderately successful small businessman—possibly a manufacturer of ladies' suits or dresses—who, at the moment, was worried about his creditors. He maintained his slumped position as they turned right on Boylston and when he spoke his gaze remained fixed.

"What happened to my boys?" he asked quietly.

"Bacon's got them under glass somewhere."

"You don't know where?"

"No."

Calenda waited while the kaleidoscopic light and darkness moved in and out of the car.

"What did they do wrong?"

"The blond got a little careless with the gun. They weren't very smart, Joe," Murdock said.

"That's the trouble." Calenda sighed. "It's hard to get smart ones these days."

"They're going to have to take the rap for what they did last night at Stacy's apartment," Murdock said. "I don't think they can beat it."

"Maybe I can make it worth their while to take it," Calenda said. "A little more trouble of that kind won't hurt too much."

"Whatever they were after must have been important."

"To me it was. . . . Take it slower, Lou," he said. "You can turn on the Avenue and come back on Commonwealth. . . . It's like this," he said to Murdock, and then waited a long time before he continued.

"I'm going to have to do a couple of years the hard way, from the looks of things. Before the revenue boys get through they'll take what they can find and maybe I'll have to do a few months more for them. But that's all right. That a guy has to expect in my business. You take chances and mostly they pay off and when they don't you figure it's the odds and you're due, or maybe you get careless and have to settle up."

He paused again, continued in the same even tones.

"I've been married thirty years," he said. "I've got about as good a wife as a man could have and two of the nicest daughters. I guess they knew what kind of business I was in and how I operated and they knew they couldn't do anything about it, so they didn't try. They took me as I was and made the best of it because I always tried to be a good husband and father when I was home. I never did much chasing around and maybe that's why I never had any trouble at home, and then last year, like a God-damned fool, I sort of went on the town."

"This was before Stacy broke that series on your rackets?" Murdock asked, wanting to keep things straight.

"Yeah. So I'm out of line—there was a woman involved —and somehow Stacy is around." He paused to curse softly and the words trailed off and he tried again. "He got a picture, but don't ask me how. I didn't know anything about it at the time. He didn't try to tap me; maybe he was scared to."

"Somebody took a shot at him later."

"Let me tell this, will you?" Calenda said, showing irritation for the first time.

Murdock found a cigarette and got a light. He leaned back and relaxed, in no hurry and not caring much whether he heard the rest of the story or not.

"Somebody took a shot at Stacy," Calenda said finally, "and Stacy figures it's one of my boys. About a day later I get this picture in the mail. I've never even seen it before and it scares the hell out of me. On the back it says —I don't remember the words—to lay off or my wife gets a copy of the photograph. That's all I know about it, and all I hear about it until the other day when I get this call. Stacy needs a half a G and I can have the negative."

Calenda grunted savagely and his voice got tight. "Well, I can't go for that standing still. I know if I pay once I'll be on the hook and I don't want to take any chances Stacy'll get cute. My wife is a jealous woman and she's loyal and she don't care about my business or if people call me a racketeer or even if I have to work out a rap. That's okay and she'll stand by. Most of what I've got left is in her name or in my daughters' names. My wife finds out about that picture and she ain't going to go for the story that it only happened once. She's gonna figure I've been cheating on her right along and she'll blow her cap. If she gets mad enough she'll talk my girls into believing what she wants 'em to believe. . . . I don't want that to happen," he said.

"If my wife pulls the string on me because of that picture I'm washed up," he added. "When I come out of

the pen I won't have a dime, and so last night I tried to
pull a fast one. I don't get what I want, so I try again this
afternoon with you."

"Why me?" Murdock said.

"You were there last night," Calenda said. "You know
about films and such. I don't know where this negative
is or even if it's still around, but I have to keep trying."
He grunted softly. "This afternoon I miss again and I
still don't know the score. That's why I wanted to talk
to you. I don't think the cops can hook up my boys or
me with that murder because we weren't in on it. It's
the picture that bothers me."

"I still don't get the angle," Murdock said.

"Maybe there ain't any," Calenda said. "I just want to
make sure. I filled you in. I want to tell you that if you
have that film, if I find out that you get cute with it for
any reason and my wife ever sees it, I can take care of
you. Even from jail I can reach back and take care of
you."

Murdock flipped his cigarette from the window, deciding that he didn't like Calenda the family man any
better than he liked Calenda the gangster. He considered
telling the man he hadn't seen the picture in question
and had no expectation of ever seeing it; then decided
he couldn't be bothered.

"Okay, Joe," he said. "I've got your message."

"I thought you would. . . . Where do you want to
get out?"

Murdock saw that they had come back downtown.
It was quieter here, darker away from the theater district. As they rolled slowly along he identified the building where Randolph Jerome had his offices and for some
reason that made him think of Martin Epps and the
grubby little office that was just around the corner; an
office which, according to Bacon, had been staked out.
On impulse, and motivated by nothing more than the

desire to have a look, Murdock said he would get out right here.

"Lou," said Calenda, and the car pulled to a stop.

Murdock got out and closed the door. "Thanks for the ride, Joe."

Calenda said nothing. When the car accelerated he was still slumped in the back seat staring straight ahead.

The street where Martin Epps had his office had all but closed down for the night. Ground-floor shop windows glowed with their night lights, but now, at eight forty-five, most of them were locked and deserted. There were a few people about and one of the radio stores was open, as was a cut-rate drugstore. The Downtown Loan Company was also doing business in accordance with the lettering on the lighted windows which said: *Open Evenings Until Nine*.

Murdock spotted the two plainclothesmen in the parked car diagonally opposite. From the street it was impossible to see the windows which opened from Epps's office and anteroom, and Murdock walked on past the entrance, remembering the narrow hall here which led to the door at the rear, wondering if it would be unlocked at this hour. He could have walked in and tried it, and the time came when he wished that he had; at the moment, however, he had another idea. If there was a back door there was probably an alley and, his curiosity getting the better of him, he walked on to the corner, turned, found the alley, and started along it.

At first the blackness seemed so complete that he could see nothing at all, so he kept to the middle, picking up his feet so he wouldn't stumble on the cobblestone surface. He had paced off the distance from the front entrance to the corner in a rough sort of way and now, recounting his steps, he came presently to this metal door which he decided was the one he sought.

Still unable to see much more than the silhouetted roof tops and the sky above, he felt along the surface of the door until he located a handle. This turned and he pulled slightly to make sure it was unlocked. That he did not enter directly was due to the fact that he was still interested in getting a look at the windows in Epps's office if he could. So he moved on down the alley for another few feet until he came to the edge of the building and the six-foot fenced-in recess between it and its neighbor. When he glanced up he saw the rectangular glow of light which marked the window of Epps's private office.

He stood a moment, puzzled, wondering about the light and the two detectives out front. When he understood that there could be several possible explanations for this, he felt his way back toward the metal door. It was not in his mind to investigate further, but the door and the hallway beyond provided a short cut to the street and now, finding the handle, he turned it.

After that Murdock never had a chance. The turning of that handle merely made it easier for the person on the other side and added to the impression that the building seemed to be falling on him.

It was all over in two seconds, but, even so, the progression had a certain clarity. He had heard nothing at all, was aware only of his thoughts. He started to pull the door toward him. There was a split instant when he had control of it. Then, in a continuation of that move, the door opened in his face to smack against him as though driven by some unseen and irresistible force.

Fortunately his hand helped break the shock of that unexpected opening, as did one knee, but only a little. The metal panel hit his forehead too as it banged open, knocking him backward and hopelessly off balance, his hat flying into space. For whoever was behind that door came through like a cyclone and was gone in the darkness as Murdock bounced against the opposite wall and fell heavily, stunned but still conscious.

The brief burst of light that came with the opening door was gone now. The blackness about him seemed complete and fathomless, and all he could hear was the sharp rap of running heels that diminished swiftly. He never did get a look at the one who had opened the door and all he knew as he rolled to one knee was that the man, silhouetted briefly against the street lights as he turned at the mouth of the alley, seemed to be tall and thin, though even this was only relative.

It took another few seconds for Murdock to understand exactly what had happened and to realize that he was not badly hurt. He came to his feet, muttering and outraged. He spent a few seconds looking for his hat and brushing himself off. Then he forgot about that and opened the door again, hurrying now because the only explanation he could find for the unseen man's wild haste was that he had held up the loan company.

This idea died as he started up the stairs. For there was no sign of excitement here and the interior seemed quiet enough except for the couple who were talking indignantly at the landing above.

"I'd just come out of the door," the woman said, still sputtering. "He almost knocked me down. If I hadn't been close to the wall he would have. Practically running, he was."

"I wish I'd seen him," the man said. "I only wish I had."

They passed Murdock without a glance and he could hear them pursuing the subject as he started along the hall, the lighted doors of the loan company on his left, turning right now into the other corridor which stood in darkness except for the dim glow near the end.

Murdock slowed down as he approached the door. He was not aware of this, nor was he aware that he was walking lightly. There was no conscious effort on his part to move with stealth, but there was an odd uncertainty working on him now in the light of what he had just heard. Instinct told him that something was wrong, but his brain had no part in the feeling, and the impression lacked conviction.

The darkened offices behind him told him that the fleeing man must have come from here and now, when the knob turned freely in his hand, he pushed on into the anteroom which stood dark and deserted. What light there was came from the open door of the private office and as he turned that way he called out:

"Hey, Epps!"

The silence around him swallowed his words, so he moved on, seeing now the littered desk and the gooseneck lamp that spotlighted it. For that first second or two as he stood in the doorway he thought the little room was empty. It was only when he moved a bit to one side that he could see why Martin Epps had not made some reply.

Murdock seemed to know in the next moment that Epps would never make any reply. Even in the shadows behind the desk, and seeing at first only the top of the mouse-colored head, he found the angle of the neck oddly crooked. By the time he had taken another step he knew that Epps must have been hit while sitting in the chair and, in falling, had pulled the chair with him so that part of it was still anchored by his twisted body.

Murdock did not touch the man. He saw that the dark stain on the shirt front was wet and still widening. A short-barreled revolver lay a foot or so from one limp hand. Over by the wall something winked at him and he realized then that the reflection came from a roundish glass paperweight about the size of a baseball.

He straightened, sucking air into his lungs and swallowing fast. A quick glance about the room told him nothing more and even as he thought of the telephone he decided against using it. Wheeling quickly, still not knowing whether Epps was alive, he strode down the hall and walked into the loan office.

There was a girl at the counter and a telephone nearby. He asked to use it and she looked at him strangely, as though startled by the pale, tight mask of his face. When she hesitated he spoke curtly:

"Police business."

That did it. She pushed the telephone toward him so fast she almost upset it; then stood watching him, her mouth sagging as he dialed the *Courier* number and asked for the Studio.

"Who's there?" he asked when Spencer answered.

"Nobody."

"Then you'll have to bring my camera over here," Murdock said, and mentioned the address. "If you get on the ball you should make it in about three minutes."

He broke the connection, dialed again. This time when he got an answer he asked for Lieutenant Bacon.

19

AL SPENCER, lugging Murdock's camera and case, beat Lieutenant Bacon by a good three minutes, but the two plainclothesmen stationed out in the car, advised by radio of the trouble, beat Spencer by two.

Luckily one of them knew Murdock slightly and, after a bit of argument, conceded that maybe Murdock should be allowed to take two photographs but that he could not send them back to the *Courier* without additional permission. Bacon, his thin face harried and lined with weariness, gave his okay almost immediately.

"Yeah, yeah," he said. "You were here first, so okay. But you stay here, understand," he added to Murdock. "You can send the shots back, if you've got anyone to take 'em, but—"

"I have," Murdock said and gestured toward the waiting Spencer.

"He got here in a hell of a hurry," Bacon said caustically.

"He's in training," Murdock said.

Spencer disappeared and Bacon knelt down by the body of Martin Epps. When he straightened he shook his head. He came over to the doorway, where Murdock was waiting, chewed silently on his lower lip a moment.

"Did you call in from here?"

"The loan office."

"You get a tip or something?"

"No."

"How did you happen to be here so quick? He's still warm."

Murdock told about his experience in the alley and as soon as he finished Bacon started in again, his tone curt and his narrowed gaze suspicious.

"What the hell were you doing in the alley anyway, for God's sake?"

Murdock thought fast because it was hard to explain an impulse and, in reality, that was about all he had to offer.

"You said you had the place staked out. I spotted the two guys in the car and I knew if I could spot them, so could Epps. I wondered if he might have used the back door, so I went into the alley to see if I could get a look at his window. I did, and it was lighted, and when I reached for the door it opened up and knocked me silly."

"That's all, hunh?" Bacon said. "You just happened to be passing by."

Murdock did not blame the lieutenant for his rough-voiced barrage because he understood how it was with Bacon. But the strain had been working on him too and his nerves were beginning to fray around the edges. In spite of himself a little of his irritation was reflected in his voice.

"If you want it all," he said, "Joe Calenda picked me up on Tremont after I'd left you. He wanted to talk and we talked and went for a ride and he let me out on the corner and I walked down here on not even a hunch; just for something to do. Maybe it was because you made a small request at dinner and I—"

"Okay, okay," said Bacon, cutting him off. "We'll talk about Calenda later." He stopped abruptly, lids drooping. "He don't figure on this, does he?"

"He and that big moose that drives for him don't figure at all. They couldn't have made it."

"Then do this for me, will you?" Bacon turned him toward the anteroom. "Go in there and sit down and be quiet and stay out of the way. Give me a half-hour or so and then we'll have a small chat about this and that."

Murdock did as directed, picking the chair in the far corner and watching the official parade into and out of the office: Bacon and Keogh and the Headquarters men, the precinct captain and his detectives, the laboratory men, the photographer, the medical examiner, and finally the removal of the blanket-covered stretcher. It was a scene he had witnessed before, with even some of the faces the same. The chief difference, aside from the victim, being the smallness of the rooms, which made the stage more crowded.

Gradually the jam thinned as tasks were finished and men were dispatched in the interests of investigative routine. Finally there were only Bacon, Keogh, and a plainclothesman who was working on the green metal filing-cabinets.

"Okay, Murdock," Bacon said. "Come on in, will you?"

Murdock figured he had been sitting there for forty minutes, the pain growing in his bruised knee and his head aching where the door had smacked it. When he stood up he found the knee was stiffening a bit and he had to limp as he walked toward the door. He had tried to think and then tried not to; he had brooded about one thing and then another until the feeling of futility and disgust began to warp his manners and his self-control. Now he gave vent to his dissatisfaction, not meaning to and a little surprised when he heard himself speak.

"Some stake-out," he said.

Bacon gave him a moment of silent appraisal.

"Just dumb cops, hunh?" he said quietly and without resentment. "Well, you could be right. You figure a thing the best way you can and even then you miss sometimes."

"Forget it," Murdock said, ashamed of himself now.

Bacon did not seem to hear him. His gaze had no focus now and he was talking more to himself than to Murdock.

"We didn't scare Epps," he said. "Didn't want him to get too nervous. We couldn't stake him out tight because the minute he tumbled he'd have started doing his business elsewhere. We wanted to see who tried to contact him, but we had to take a chance on that too."

"Look," Murdock said. "I was out of line. Let it go, will you, please?"

Bacon heard him this time. He looked over at Keogh and then at the man who was busy with the files. When he got ready he gave Murdock a wry grin to show he hadn't lost his sense of humor.

"I'm practicing," he said. "I'm going to have to do some explaining for what happened tonight, so see how I sound. . . . We want to know who comes to see Epps, either here or at his apartment," he said. "We can't start

checking everybody who comes in that door downstairs
—even if we wanted to—not with that loan office open until nine at night. We're not even interested in the building or the people; not until Epps himself shows. That's
what those two men outside were waiting for: Epps.
When he shows, the time comes to move in close and
see what we can see. We know he may spot the plant,
but it's a chance we got to take because we're damn
sure he'll spot anybody trying to cover the back door."

He shrugged his square shoulders and tipped his hat
back. "So he outsmarts us and himself. He tries the back
way and it's uncovered. He must have phoned somebody
—or somebody phoned him—and he told them to come
the back way. Very simple. My guys sit out front gabbing
and wearing out the seat of their pants and Epps has
a date with a killer. Whoever it was slugged him with
the paperweight and then took his gun to finish the job."

"Epps's gun?"

"Sure. We checked the number against the permit.
. . . You're sure you didn't get a look at the guy who
knocked you over?" he said. "You didn't see him until
he hit the end of the alley, but he looked thin and maybe
tall, is that it?"

Murdock nodded and Bacon turned to the desk,
pointing to the personal objects that had been emptied
from Epps's pockets.

"There're just two things here that look like something," he said. "This is the first one. It was in his wallet
and you'll see it's dated the day before yesterday."

Murdock took the check that Bacon offered him. He
had an idea about the signature, and he was right. Made
out to Martin Epps in the amount of one hundred dollars,
it was signed by Randolph Jerome.

"That," said Bacon, "and this." He took an envelope
from his pocket and spread the contents on the desk
while Murdock's eyes fastened on the thin, folded stack

of new fifty-dollar bills. "Thirty-eight bucks in old bills and nine new fifties. Not in this envelope; in his wallet. As a guess, he cracked one of the fifties, meaning that originally there were ten. So where would a punk like Epps get five hundred bucks? My guess is he never earned that big a fee in his life."

Murdock made the expected reply. "So somebody paid him off either yesterday or today," he said, knowing where the money had come from, but for some reason that was not clear even to him unwilling to say it was Vivian Jerome who had made that payment. Eventually Bacon was going to question her and she would have to tell him a story, and if she felt it necessary to tell him about the money she had given to Stacy she would do so.

"You'd think," he said, "that if the person that paid Epps killed him he might also pick up the money. You'd think that if Jerome killed him he'd stop to look for his check."

"Maybe you would," Bacon said. "But not me. It don't follow, son. The bills and that check weren't kicking around on top of the desk, you know. They were tucked in the wallet. Jerome dated that check two days ago. Why would he think Epps hadn't already cashed it?"

He shook his head. "No. Somebody comes down here, maybe knowing he's going to kill and maybe not. That we can't tell about because something could have happened here to make it a spur-of-the-moment job. Kill a man like this and you're not going to hang around and take the chance that someone will walk in on you unless you're looking for a very special thing. If the killer is the one who made the payment, how does he know Epps hasn't banked it or stuck it away some place? No," he said again and now exasperation began to color his words.

"What the hell does that check prove?" he demanded

and then answered himself. "Only that Jerome hired Epps for some little job. With Epps gone nobody but Jerome is going to say what that job was, and not even then if he don't want to. The check proves nothing without corroborating evidence."

"Have you talked to him?" Murdock asked.

"I haven't had time since dinner," Bacon said. "I phoned him and asked him if he would stop in this evening and he said he would. Before he showed up I had to run out on this thing."

He put his hat back on the center of his head and said: "About the only thing we're sure of is that you were right about seeing Epps last night. We don't know when the Jerome woman left or if her husband showed and, if he did, whether he went calling on Stacy or not."

"Epps knew."

"Hah!" said Bacon. "Epps made the mistake of underestimating a killer. He must have hung around outside Stacy's and finally saw something that smelled to him and went up and had a look—the door was on latch, remember? I think he found Stacy and ducked out, pretty sure by then who had done the job. My guess is he's the guy that tipped us off."

"If Stacy had the five hundred on him—he'd been collecting, remember—would Epps have taken a quick look and grabbed it?"

Bacon threw his hands wide and let them drop. He began to button his coat. "My God!" he said. "How do I know? Two killings and I still don't know." He paused, jaw tightening. "But it's early yet. . . . Let's go, Sergeant," he said to Keogh. "We've got work to do."

Murdock went straight back to the *Courier*, detouring past the Studio to make sure the film he had exposed in Epps's office had been processed and printed before he went upstairs. Here the city editor greeted him with enthusiasm, saying nice things about the pictures and asking if he could help with a story. Murdock said he could and went over and sat down with Murray, a veteran rewrite man, supplying what information he could.

All this took no more than ten minutes, and when he finished he went downstairs and took a cab to the Band Box. The little brunette who had taken Nancy Larkin's place gave him a cute smile, but he wrestled his hat away from her, saying that he was only going into the bar for a minute.

It was then after eleven o'clock and the entertainer must have just finished her stint, because the bandstand was dark and there was no sign of Frost's trio. There were no more than a dozen couples in the main room and only two stags at the bar, a middle-aged pair who sat quietly staring at their drinks like men who had been allowed a night out and wished they were home. Murdock moved to the far end of the bar and Harry came toward him, polishing a glass.

"No music, Harry?" Murdock asked.

"Like last night," Harry said, "you're a little late, Mr. Murdock. We had music earlier," he said. "Then we got a repeat performance."

Murdock let his arched brows ask a question.

"They put the arm on Jack again," Harry said. "Same two dicks."

"How long ago?"

"Oh, maybe a half-hour. Can I make you something?"

Murdock thought it over and shook his head. He said one wouldn't do him any good and if he took two he might want three and that would be worse.

Harry nodded. "You look all in," he said. "What you need is a hot bath and maybe a good slug before you get into bed."

Harry's suggestion stuck in Murdock's mind as he rode home, and when he went upstairs he decided it was excellent advice. Normally a shower man, he had an idea that for tonight a hot tub would be best, not only because it would relax him more but because it might soak some of the stiffness out of his knee.

With this in mind he checked the night lock on the door and then went over to flip the switch on the telephone so that it would not ring until he was ready for it. Out in the kitchen he put a saucepan on to heat some water and then went into the bathroom to start his tub.

When he had stripped he examined his knee and explored the bluish swelling with gentle fingers. A glance in a mirror showed a mark on his forehead, but he thought this was mostly dirt, so he turned away to hang up his suit, satisfied that he could wear it at least once more before having it pressed. Donning robe and slippers, he went back to the kitchen and brought out a jar of instant coffee and a bottle of his good brandy. With the water boiling, he made his coffee, laced it generously with brandy, and then went into the bath again. He took a swallow of his brew and put the cup on the bath stool and then slid slowly into the tub, wincing as the heat hit his knee.

For a man who was mentally discouraged and physically spent the treatment proved to be excellent therapy. For when, a few minutes later, he climbed into bed and turned out the light he fell asleep almost at once.

20

WHEN KENT MURDOCK wakened at five minutes of nine the next morning the sunshine was streaming through the window and spreading a bright, warm carpet over the foot of his bed. He lay on his back, and in those first luxurious moments that came with returning consciousness he stretched full-length under the covers, catlike and comfortable. Reluctant to do more than this, he relaxed for a minute or two, and as his mind began to work he felt his knee. When he found it less tender he flexed it cautiously until he was sure it was not going to bother him.

With the covers thrown back he sat on the edge of the bed a second or two to arch his back and tense his arm and shoulder muscles and then, because it surprised him that he should feel so good, he grinned, some wordless sound of satisfaction, animal-like in its inflection, rising in his throat as he stepped over to close the window. When he had put his pajamas aside he found his slippers and went naked into the kitchen to put some water on for coffee.

In the bathroom he brushed his teeth and rinsed his mouth, and he was just pulling out his shaving things when the sound of the buzzer shattered his mood and brought him up short.

Swearing softly, he glanced into the mirror. He scowled and the image scowled back at him to show a tousle-headed man with a lean, angular face that had become suddenly unhappy, and sober dark eyes.

"No," he said as the buzzer again rasped out its insistent demand. "I'm damned if I will."

He reached for his shaving-cream, uncapped it. For another second or two the stubbornness held him, but when the sound came for the third time he wheeled and went into the bedroom to snatch up his robe.

Crossing the living-room with the buzzer still rasping on its third and uninterrupted summons, he belted his robe, hurrying now as he began to mutter profane imprecations. The room went suddenly quiet as he reached for the door. He turned the bolt and the knob and yanked. Then he was staring at the blonde, bareheaded girl who waited there.

Nancy Larkin did not wait for an invitation to enter, but stepped swiftly across the threshold, sweeping past Murdock as he moved aside. She said nothing at all, nor did Murdock, until he had closed the door and moved up to confront her. Even then she did not seem to see him. Her blue eyes had a faraway look and her hands kept working on the front of her coat as she kept wrapping it more tightly about her.

"They've arrested Jack." The words came out stiff and jerky and she spoke like an automaton, without regard for grammar or sequence. "They came for him last night. They took me too, but I couldn't tell them anything more and they sent me home at one o'clock, but they kept Jack. I went there this morning and they wouldn't let me see him. I have to get a lawyer and I don't know who to get and—"

She suddenly ran out of words and of breath, and while the things she said came as no great surprise to Murdock he found himself wondering who it was that Nancy cared most for: Stacy or Jack Frost.

Instinct and experience told him that right now the girl needed another kind of help. Her young face looked white and rigid, and hysteria was building in the corners of her eyes as they started to fill. He did not ask her why she had come or what she wanted. Instead, believing bluntness more effective than sympathy, he snapped at her.

"Cut it out!" he said.

"What?" she said, blinking.

"It's no good crying. Take your coat off." He reached for it, shaking her gently in the process. "Pull yourself together. Have you had breakfast?"

"No—I—"

"I've got water on the stove," he said. "There's a jar

of instant coffee on the counter and if you look around you'll find a couple of cups."

"I don't want anything," she said, lips trembling, but listening now to what he said.

"Well, I do," Murdock said. "There's frozen orange juice in the icebox. Do you know how to fix it?"

"Of course I do."

"All right, then fix two orange juices and two coffees. Bring 'em in here when you finish. I've got to shave and put on some clothes."

He did not give her a chance to argue, but turned abruptly and walked quickly into the bedroom, closing the door behind him. When he finished shaving he combed his hair and put on clean shorts. From the closet he took gray slacks and an odd Shetland jacket, selected a blue Oxford shirt with a button-down collar and a plain maroon tie. All of this took him about five minutes and when he went back to the living-room Nancy was waiting, the coffee and orange juice standing on a tray.

A quick glance told Murdock she was already better. There was a touch of color in her cheeks and for the moment her eyes were dry as he busied himself with his orange juice and stirred his coffee.

"I would have made you some toast," she said in simple apology, "but there wasn't any bread."

"It gets stale on me," Murdock said. "I don't use enough of it. . . . Finish your coffee and then tell me why you don't think Jack should be arrested."

She kept sipping her coffee and watching him over the brim of the cup. She seemed to be considering her answer and when it came her tone was quietly defiant.

"Because he didn't kill Ralph," she said. "He couldn't have. Not deliberately like that. I don't even think he owned a gun."

"He had a blackjack."

"I know. And I can understand him trying to use it

and maybe, if he started, hitting Ralph too hard or something like that." She put her cup down and sat straight
on the edge of her chair, her hands in her lap and her
small chin up. "He was drunk and he was jealous and I
know he wanted to hurt Ralph, but—"

"You were pretty scared about what might happen,"
Murdock cut in. "You left the Band Box to warn Stacy."

"Because I didn't want any trouble. I knew Jack
would be all right again once he sobered up and I ran
home and called Ralph's apartment and there wasn't any
answer and I thought he might just possibly have stopped
to see his wife and I tried there and then I called the
Courier and they couldn't tell me when he'd be back.
I was almost frantic when I tried the apartment again."

"That time he answered," Murdock said, "and you
talked him into coming to your place."

She nodded and began to tell the same story she had
told Lieutenant Bacon the first night: She wanted Stacy
to stay away from his apartment. She felt to blame for
what had happened, and why couldn't Stacy be sensible
and stay out of Frost's way until he realized what he
was doing? Stacy had refused to be alarmed. He could
handle Frost and he wasn't going to run. . . .

She went on, repeating herself in her earnestness, but
Murdock no longer heard her because he was thinking
back, remembering things, some of which Nancy Larkin
did not know. He saw now that there was no point in
telling her what had happened to Martin Epps, or that
he knew Epps had telephoned Frost the previous day.
Instead he told her to relax while he called Bacon and
tried to find out just what the score was.

Bacon was in, but he was busy and he said so im-
patiently. "This is my busy day, kid," he said, "so make
it snappy."

"I hear you're holding Frost."

"You're damn right we're holding him."

"That must mean you've got something new," Murdock said. "What?"

"Just enough," Bacon said, "with what we already had. We already had the motive, because Frost was mad and jealous and drunk and he went looking for Stacy. His alibi isn't worth a damn and my beagles turned up something that gives him the opportunity. Remember the television that was going upstairs in the flat above Stacy?" he said.

"Well, these characters are fans. Have it on every night. Get people in to watch with them and furnish cake and coffee. They had company that night. Another couple. Turned the set off at ten thirty and they think it was about ten minutes later when the company left. They came downstairs—the company I mean—as Frost started up, and they remembered him because he was a stranger and acted a little drunk. When we showed them a picture they said yes, so my beagles brought 'em down last night after we'd picked up Frost and the couple made it positive. So that gives us motive and opportunity, and on top of that we got a break last night. It's not evidence in the Stacy killing, but it supports what we have. . . . You think the guy that knocked you down with the door was tall and thin, right?"

"I thought he was," Murdock said, aware that the description was perfect for Frost, "but it was only an impression."

"Well, this isn't. Frost's car was parked about a half-block from the entrance to that alley. We got the break because he must have parked in a hurry and not too good. The back end of the wagon was sticking out in the street and this beat man out of the precinct stopped to look at it. This is around five minutes of nine and he's wondering should he slap a ticket on it when up comes Frost on the double. He talks the cop out of it, saying he'd only left it there a couple minutes, but our man had sense enough to ask for the license and Frost had to produce it. Later the cop remembered."

"What does Frost say?"

"He ain't talking."

"Does he deny going to Stacy's place that night?"

"I'm telling you," Bacon said shortly, "he ain't talking. If he opens his mouth he's cooked and he probably knows it. We still have some pieces we'd like to fill in, but the D.A.'s satisfied. He'll be asking for an indictment next week and if you ask me I think it'll stick."

Murdock walked over to the window when he hung up. He knew the girl had heard every word, that she was watching him intently and waiting for some reaction, but after a bit he forgot about her and stood motionless as some new concentration gripped him.

His face was somberly set and staring fixedly, but not at anything in the street outside. The things he saw were in his mind and they grew clearer as he began to examine them anew. Yesterday he had spent most of his time chasing around and asking questions without making any real effort to analyze and co-ordinate things he already knew. Now everything was different. There was a small springboard under him where none had been before, and with its buoyant lift remembered things came back, demanding answers. Most of the facts had been there for him almost from the beginning and now, his brain focused on a heretofore hidden channel, he found a pattern emerging that was already making sense.

Nancy Larkin could not have known what he was thinking, but she must have sensed his mood, for she remained quite still, asking no questions as she sat there and the silent minutes ticked off. When she could stand it no longer she rose and went quietly out to the kitchen with the tray. She rinsed the cups and glasses. She dried them carefully and then came back to sit down exactly as she had been before. Only when Murdock turned toward her did she speak.

"What did they say?"

"They know that Jack went to Stacy's," Murdock said, interrupting her when she seemed about to speak. "He was seen coming up the stairs and we know the door was unlocked, so we have to assume that he went in."

"But—" she protested in quick alarm.

"It's just a question of whether Stacy was dead by that time or not."

"Then he was," she said quickly, her trust unshaken. "He must have been."

Murdock sighed and went over to her as she came to her feet. He stood close, not touching her, smiling just a little because he was moved by her courage and her stubborn faith in a man who already had two strikes on him. For a moment he wondered if this faith was prompted simply by loyalty toward one who had been kind to her when she needed help, or whether underneath it all there was a love that had never been realized, even by her. Then, because he knew it made no difference, he said:

"You think that because that's what you want to think."

She looked up at him with wide-open eyes that were beginning to gather moisture. Her mouth trembled.

"It could be true, couldn't it?" she asked.

"Yes, it could be true," Murdock said. "You could be right, and maybe with some luck we can prove it."

She put her head down then and suddenly she leaned against him, her face buried in the hollow of his shoulder. When he put his arms around her to support her he could feel the shudder run through her slender body and he waited a minute to give her a chance to regain her self-control.

"It's only an idea," he said. "There may be nothing

to it, but I'll give it a try. . . . Look," he said, holding her away from him. "Why don't you stay here for the day so I'll know where you are? Can you?"

"Why—yes."

"You don't have to lock yourself in or anything and you'll have to go out for lunch. But there's plenty to read here and if you like music you'll find all kinds of records. Go wash your face and put on some make-up," he said and turned her away. "I've got a couple of phone calls to make."

21

IT WAS nine thirty when Nancy Larkin went into the bathroom to give her young face a beauty treatment, and when the door closed Murdock sat down beside the telephone, remembering MacGrath's suggestion about using the brains the *Courier* had to offer and considering briefly the staff men who might best serve his purpose.

He needed help and if the idea that had so recently begun to blossom in the back of his head had any merit he would need two helpers besides himself. Taking into account the particular sort of assignment he had in mind, he finally settled on two veterans who had consistently proved both resourceful and ingenious. His problem then was to sell them the idea of some extra work, since they were not due at the office until later in the day.

He did not have to do much selling when he told them he was acting on a suggestion of T. A. MacGrath. Both said they could meet him, so he mentioned a coffee shop round the corner from the *Courier* and told them to make it as soon as they could.

Murdock was getting his hat and coat out of the hall

closet when Nancy Larkin came out of his room. The time-out had done her a lot of good. Her blue eyes seemed brighter and she carried her slenderness with more confidence as she came toward him. She wore a little too much make-up for Murdock's taste, but she did not look cheap and he understood that its main purpose was one of morale.

When she saw what he was doing she took the coat and held it for him. Then as he slipped into it she turned him toward her, took his lapels in her hands, and, coming quickly up on tiptoes, kissed him full on the mouth.

"Please try hard," she said. "I'll be waiting."

Murdock tasted strawberry lipstick on his way downstairs, but somehow the gesture pleased him because it was so simply and genuinely done. As a precautionary measure lest he be subjected to some ribald comments later on, he wiped his lips with his handkerchief as he came out on the sidewalk, grinning a little self-consciously as he noticed the carmine smear on the clean linen. Then, because he would need a car, he started toward his garage two blocks away.

Neither of the newsmen were at the coffee shop when Murdock arrived, so he went into the telephone booth and made two calls. He was on the second one when Ed Gates came in, spotted him, waved, and sat down at a table by the wall. A graying, bespectacled man of fifty or so, Gates had covered nearly every beat in the city during his career with the *Courier*, and, though in recent years he had settled for a desk, there remained in the back of his mind all of the tricks of the trade he had learned in former years.

Lee Chadwick, who joined them a minute or two later, was a lank and somewhat untidy forty-five-year-old bachelor. He had worked for the *Courier* for twenty of those years and seldom wrote anything more than his name, and certain vital statistics of those who crossed his path. He was usually broke and often drank a little too much, but, for all of that, he was a dependable leg-man and his inventiveness and perspicacity had high ratings in the various city rooms.

Over their coffee Murdock told his two helpers what he wanted without telling them exactly why. The two telephone calls he had made while waiting had been to the post office and a substation, but even so his infor-mation was sketchy and vague.

"I don't know how long it'll take," he said. "We'll just have to wait it out."

"The mail will be delivered first," Gates said, glancing at his watch. "Maybe already delivered."

"That's why we've got to get started," Murdock said. "But I don't think a mailman will be carrying the sort of thing I have in mind. The parcel-post man is probably the man we want, but there's no telling when he'll show up."

"Check me," Chadwick said. "I take a plant at the Riverside where this Mrs. Jerome lives. I wait until I see if a package is delivered, which may take hours, so what excuse do I have for hanging around? It's sort of a high-class joint."

"Tell them you're doing a survey on what the tenants think of rent control." Murdock grinned. "How do I know? I should be telling you how to operate?"

Chadwick grunted to show he appreciated the com-pliment. "I'll think of something."

"All I can do," Gates said wryly, "is sort of patrol the hall where Randolph Jerome has his office, like I'm wait-ing to meet someone. That's going to be a lot of standing for a desk man. . . . So if a package is delivered, then what?"

"If you could get a look at it, fine," Murdock said, "but don't crowd it. The main thing is just to find out if a package is delivered today for either Jerome or his wife."

"Suppose one is. What'll you be doing?"

"The same thing you are, in another spot."

"What we need," said Chadwick, "is a two-way radio hook-up."

"Call the office," Murdock said. "It's all you can do. Leave word with the operator and I'll call in to check when I can."

"If either Lee or I spot this package," Gates said slowly, "you figure to check on it later? What makes you think it will still be there?"

"It's a chance I have to take. We're entitled to a little luck."

"What's behind this?" Chadwick asked. "Or is this top secret for button-pushers only?"

"Stacy." Murdock picked up the checks. "I hope."

"Stacy?" Gates frowned. "The Jeromes are mixed up with Stacy?"

Murdock made no reply and Chadwick said quietly: "Stacy was a thief, wasn't he?"

The remark surprised Murdock, though he did not know why. He looked at Gates. "What do you think?"

"I didn't like him much," Gates said. "That's all I know."

"Where did you get the idea, Lee?" Murdock said.

"I've been around longer than you have." Chadwick hesitated, his eyes wise, sardonic, and a little bloodshot. "It's a hunch I had," he said. "The trouble with you is you've been spending too much time behind a desk these last few years. . . . Was he?" he added.

"What?"

"A thief?"

"Yes."

"Okay." Chadwick pushed his chair back. "Then leave us get started, men."

Kent Murdock had to drive around the block once before he could find a parking-space in the block where Elinor Stacy lived and this put him about a hundred feet from the entrance of the five-story building. With the children in school the street was quiet, with only two baby carriages in sight. Housewives came and went with their market baskets and bags and no one paid any attention to Murdock when he stepped into the foyer to see if any mail had been delivered. Assured that the recessed wall boxes were empty, he went back to the car and began to read his paper.

The mailman came swinging along the street about twenty minutes later and Murdock timed his approach so that he came into the foyer as the mailman finished his distribution. There was no package in sight and none that he could see in the sack.

"You don't deliver packages?" Murdock asked.

"Only first-class," the mailman said. "The parcel-post guys come around later."

Murdock went back to his car. For another half-hour he read the newspaper and then he got out and came down the street to reconnoiter round the corner. Spotting the delicatessen in the middle of the block with a blue-and-white sign of a pay station over the door, he hurried to it and telephoned the *Courier*. When the operator told him there had been no word from either Gates or Chadwick he returned to the car.

That particular copy of the *Courier* had a more thorough reading than any Murdock had looked at for years. He read practically everything in it as time dragged on, skipping only the menus on the home-making page and then starting on the crossword puzzle.

Twelve o'clock came, and with it a few smaller children straggled down the street to their respective homes, apparently finished with their schooling for the day. One o'clock saw the puzzle completed except for one corner which defied him. He gave up finally and put the paper aside, aware of a growing hunger but afraid to leave his post. Two o'clock and then, some time after that, a green truck swung into the street and stopped just short of the corner.

A package went into the brownstone on the opposite side of the street. Two more were delivered to the four-story apartment house two doors away. The truck came slowly toward Murdock to stop across from him, double-parking while the driver made the last delivery in the block to a three-story red-brick apartment house. There was nothing for the building where Elinor Stacy lived, but Murdock waited until the truck had turned the corner before hurrying back to the delicatessen. This time when he dialed his number there was news for him.

"Yes, Mr. Murdock," the *Courier* operator said. "Mr. Chadwick said to tell you there was no package. Mr. Gates called in to say that there *was* a package and that he would be waiting for you. . . . Oh, yes. There was one other message. A Miss Hargrove wants you to have dinner at her place tonight and unless you call her she'll expect you at seven."

Betty Hargrove?

The thought of her made Murdock grin as he hung up and there was a brief instant of happy contemplation before he stifled the warm glow of anticipation and considered the job at hand. After that it took him about seven minutes to drive to this building where Randolph Jerome had his office, and he parked close by in a restricted area, hoping that the press card he took from the glove compartment and propped against the windshield might prevent the car from being tagged. Business was slack in the lobby at that hour. The clerk behind the cigar counter sat on his stool and gazed with bored indifference at the revolving door, and the elevator starter was chatting with one of his operators next to

an empty car. Murdock stepped inside and the seconds
ticked by until the conference ended and the operator
strolled into the car and closed the door.

Ed Gates was perched on the window sill at the far
end of the corridor and when he spotted Murdock he
rose slowly and came forward with labored steps and a
look of relief on his bespectacled face.

"This sort of work is for younger men," he said. "I
haven't got the arches for it."

"What sort of package?"

"Oh—like so." Gates pantomimed an object with his
hands to indicate a parcel perhaps twelve by sixteen
inches. "Also two or three large manila envelopes."

"How long ago?"

"It seems like four years." Gates glanced at his watch.
"About an hour, maybe."

"I phoned in as soon as I could."

"Sure, that's okay. Can you take it from here?"

Murdock said he could, but as he watched Gates move
down toward the elevators he realized that this was a
gross overstatement. Analyzing more thoroughly, he was
also aware that the mere fact that a package had been
delivered to Randolph Jerome meant nothing in itself.
To mean anything this had to be a particular package
and even if this was the case any number of things might
have happened to that package in the hour since delivery.

The more he thought about it, the more discouraged
he became until, in the end, he deliberately put such
considerations from his mind, knowing that what he
needed most was a bit of luck. For if his idea and his
hunch were to pay off he had to locate this package, get
a look at it, and, if possible, see how it was addressed.

It was a large order and he knew it as he opened the
door and started across the anteroom. The same pleasant-
mannered brunette rose to meet him. Murdock took his

hat off. He smiled at her and said: "Good afternoon," and kept right on walking toward the closed door of Jerome's private office, eyes busy all the time and seeing no sign here of a package such as Gates had described. Aware now of his intention, the girl faltered and her face looked dismayed and a little hurt at this display of rudeness and bad manners. She tried to stop him in a hesitant sort of way even as she realized she could not quite catch up to him.

"Mr. Jerome is busy," she said. "If you'll wait here I'll—"

"I'll only be a minute," Murdock said and now, another step taking him to the door, he turned the knob and moved inside.

The luck that Murdock so earnestly hoped for split down the middle for him, the bad part taking the form of another caller whose presence would forestall any attempt to talk much to Jerome; the good part was the package, which sat on a corner of the desk, almost completely covered by two large manila envelopes.

Randolph Jerome was dressed in a neatly pressed gray flannel suit, a tattersall vest, and a bow tie. Annoyance clouded his tanned face as he recognized Murdock and exchanged glances with his visitor, an older man in a dark suit and topcoat who sat at one end of the desk.

"I'm sorry to barge in like this," Murdock began.

"Then why did you?" Jerome said coldly.

"I wanted to ask if you knew about Jack Frost." Murdock was at the desk now, disappointment striking at him as he realized that the two envelopes on top of the package would prevent him from learning much about it. At the very top he could see the long line of three-cent stamps, but there seemed to be no return address in the upper left-hand corner. Short of reaching over and picking the package up, a move which seemed unwise just then, he had to be content with knowing that his hunch was still valid.

"Yes, I know about Frost," Jerome said, color rising in his cheeks and his hands clenched on the chair arms.

"You talked with Bacon?"

"Last night," Jerome said. "And I have nothing further to say to you, now or any other time."

He stood up, swung round the edge of the desk, and strode over to the door. He opened it, his gaze narrowed and the angle of his solid jaw belligerent. The gesture and his attitude as he stood holding the door open suggested that it was time for Murdock to go unless he wanted to run the risk of being tossed out. Murdock accepted the invitation.

"Okay," he said, his grin tight. "Just thought I'd check, Mr. Jerome."

There was no traffic ticket on Murdock's car when he returned to it, so he put his press card away and drove westward and away from the downtown congestion until he found a small restaurant where he could park. He ordered a ham-and-cheese sandwich and coffee, and while he ate he considered the alternatives left to him. As he examined again the mental pattern he had been working on he felt it was the right one and had a sound basis in fact. For all of that he still had to prove the theory, and by the time he had finished his coffee and a cigarette he knew what he had to do. If he was wrong he'd make his apologies as best he could; if he was right it would be time for Lieutenant Bacon.

The cashier gave him some change and he stepped into the telephone booth and made three quick calls, one of which was to Elinor Stacy, who said yes, she was home and would be glad to see him.

22

WHEN ELINOR STACY opened the door for Murdock a few minutes later he was at once aware of a subtle change in her appearance. He did not know just why he thought so, because as she greeted him pleasantly and asked him to come in he could find no specific physical difference.

His earlier impression—that it seemed unlikely she would ever be pointed out for her beauty—remained unchanged, but somehow her face seemed more rested and at ease, was quicker to smile. Her brown hair still had no great style, but it had a softer look, she wore a bit of lipstick to give her mouth the needed color, and her intelligent, well-spaced eyes were, in themselves, both striking and pretty. Her navy wool dress lacked distinction, but it occurred to him again that with the proper advice and a judicious application of the beauty aids that other women used she could be more than reasonably attractive.

"Let me take your coat and hat," she said. "Would you like a drink?" she added when she had put his things aside. "Or perhaps a cup of tea?"

Murdock thanked her and said no. He said he couldn't stay long but he wanted to ask her if her lawyer had located any additional assets, particularly cash, that her husband might have left.

"No," she said, sobering, "he hasn't."

"Do you know about Jack Frost?"

She nodded and picked up a folded newspaper. "Only what it says here, that the police have arrested him in Ralph's murder." She frowned, put the paper aside, and

then sat down on the couch. "I never even knew there
was such a man until a few days ago. He's the one that
Nancy Larkin used to go with, isn't he? And the police
think he killed Ralph because he was jealous. Is that it?"

"That's the way it looks. They think he also killed a
private detective named Martin Epps," Murdock said.
"There's a story on that too," he added and pointed to
the picture he had taken.

"I read it." The frown grew and her gaze seemed perplexed. "But it doesn't say anything there about that
having anything to do with Ralph."

"The police didn't give out that theory when the paper
went to press." Murdock glanced at his watch to find
that he had only been here six minutes. "The police know
Frost went to Ralph's apartment and they think Epps
knew this and made the mistake of telling Frost or trying to collect for a promise of silence."

He paused to light a cigarette and went on to add
details, speaking slowly and taking his time, worrying a
little as the minutes passed, the impatience growing in
him as he began to run out of words.

In the beginning Elinor Stacy listened with interest,
but gradually she seemed to sense that he was not at
ease. She sat quietly, her light-blue eyes more puzzled
than curious now, still polite, but making no attempt to
draw him out.

Finally she said: "Are you sure you wouldn't like a
drink?"

Murdock put out his cigarette and was about to accept, if only to give himself an excuse to stay awhile
longer, when the knock came at the door. Elinor Stacy
turned from the hips to look at it; then she rose and
walked across the room. Murdock was on his feet too,
mentally crossing his fingers as his interest quickened
and an odd feeling of suspense began to infilter his
thoughts. Only when the door opened and he saw Ran-

dolph Jerome standing in the hall could he relax and consider what the next step should be.

"Hello, Elinor," Jerome said, not yet aware of Murdock.

"Why, Mr. Jerome," the woman said. "Come in, won't you? It's nice of you to—"

"Hello, Mr. Jerome," Murdock said.

"Here, let me take those."

Elinor Stacy reached for the familiar-looking brown-paper package and the briefcase Jerome carried. He was inside now, hat in hand as the woman put the things on the little table just inside the room, but he made no attempt to advance. He gave Murdock a long, distasteful look and his voice was unpleasant.

"I didn't expect to find you here," he said, "but what I told you in my office still goes." He glanced at the woman. "I'll just run along," he said.

"You'd better come in," Murdock said levelly. "I've already phoned Lieutenant Bacon. He wasn't in, but I left word and I imagine he'll be around before too long."

Elinor looked from one to the other, her brow furrowing as she sensed the animosity between the two men. She reached for Jerome's hat and he let go of it absently and she put it aside.

"Did you expect Mr. Jerome to come here?" she said, turning to Murdock.

"Yes," Murdock said. "I phoned him a few minutes before I got here."

"*You* phoned me?" Jerome said, hard glints showing in his steady eyes. "Oh," he said, "so that's it." He glanced at the woman. "A man telephoned me about a half-hour ago and represented himself as your attorney—"

Murdock cut him off. "I found out that package was delivered to your office this morning."

"Package?" Elinor Stacy said.

"That one," Murdock said, pointing. "That's why I barged in on you this morning," he added to Jerome.

"To see if it was there?"

"I've got a theory on that package." Murdock kept his attention on Jerome. "I think you ought to hear it, but it may take a little time. Why don't we all sit down?"

Jerome seemed about to rebel. "I'm not so sure I—"

He did not finish the thought. He watched Elinor Stacy move back to the couch and sit on the edge of it. Finally, still truculent and suspicious, he reached for a straight-backed chair and pulled it toward him. He sat down stiffly, his gaze challenging. Murdock ignored it and took the rocking-chair opposite. When he spoke his tone was quietly aggressive, reflecting an outward confidence he did not feel.

"Before we get on the package," he said, "I'd like to ask if the police told you about the nine new fifty-dollar bills that were found in Epps's wallet."

"Yes," Jerome said.

"Have you any idea where Epps got them?"

"None."

"Your wife got ten new fifties from the bank the day Stacy was killed. She put them in an envelope and gave them to Stacy that night and—"

Jerome cut him off, coldly and in his somewhat stilted way of speaking. "I have no intention of discussing my wife with you," he said, "or listening to any theory concerning her."

"Okay," Murdock said. "I'm just trying to get some things straightened out in my mind." He leaned back, brows warping as his concentration developed. "When I went to Stacy's apartment the night he was killed," he said, "there was a package for him which contained three shirts. He showed them to me and took them into the bedroom and he threw the box, paper, and string at the wastebasket which stood near the desk. When I went back after the murder a detective was going through that basket for possible leads and the box and paper were no longer there. I noticed it at the time, but not until this morning when I discovered something else that gave me a new slant on things, not until then did I remember about the box and paper and begin to wonder what had happened.

"There was just one other thing I noticed that night that had changed between my first and second trips to the apartment," he said, hesitating now because he did not want to speak of Betty Hargrove and his forced journey through the apartment while she held the gun. "I happened to know the door to the closet in Stacy's bedroom was locked at the time he was away calling on Nancy Larkin. Later the door was open."

"What about it?" Jerome asked.

"It suggested to me that Stacy had some valuables in there and yet the police found nothing to substantiate the idea. What they did discover the following day was that Stacy had visited his safe-deposit box and turned in the keys."

He glanced at the woman. "Bacon had a theory on that. He thought your husband was getting ready to leave town. He said it was his idea that he was going to leave with or without Nancy Larkin."

"I wouldn't have put it past him," she said woodenly.

"But Nancy had no idea about that. He didn't say anything to her about running away, so my guess is that he was going by himself. He gave the girl a lot of time, but I doubt if he was really in love with her."

"I don't think he ever loved anyone, really," she said.

"We do know," Murdock continued, "that he had been collecting money from people for the past two or three years and that he was trying to get his hands on a little more the last week or so. Now you were going to divorce him."

"Yes."

"Your lawyer wanted to know what Stacy had so he could work out some property settlement."

"That's right," she replied without inflection.

"But up until the afternoon of the murder Stacy hadn't told the lawyer anything. You told me that the other day."

"Yes, because it's true."

"But Stacy did clean out the box and the police haven't been able to find out that he rented another one someplace else, so my guess is he brought the contents home and locked it in his closet until he was ready to skip."

He rose quickly, stepped over to the table, and slid the package from under the briefcase. A glance at it told him that this part of his theory was right, but the discovery brought no real sense of satisfaction; instead he was aware only of the stillness of the room and the pull of some new tension across his chest.

"The way to find out if my idea is right," he said, "is to open this."

Jerome leaned forward, his tanned face tight and his shoulders hunched.

"Are you trying to say that that package contains whatever of value was in Stacy's closet? The things he had taken from his safe-deposit box?"

"I am saying it."

"Is that a guess?"

"Not entirely." Murdock held the parcel up so the front of it was visible, pointing now to the long strip of three-cent stamps across the top. "I saw those stamps in your office," he said. "That told me the package was never mailed in a post office."

Jerome, not as quick as he might have been, said: "Why?"

"Because in a post office the clerks generally use as few stamps as possible. They get the proper amount by using stamps of a higher denomination. Whoever put those stamps on used more than he needed for the weight of the package because he had to be sure it carried enough postage, and he did not mail it at the general post office because, if he had, it would have been delivered yesterday."

He took a breath and said: "I checked with the nearest substation. It's not open evenings, but there's a mailbox outside. The last collection is at eight thirty at night and none then until eight the next morning. First-class mail posted at night and picked up in the morning would most likely be delivered, at least in the central part of town, that same day, though I could get no positive assurance even on that. But parcel post takes another day."

"But even so," Jerome protested.

"That isn't all," Murdock said, interrupting. "If I'm right this wrapping-paper will have the label of the haberdashery shop on the inside—I think it was Anderson's. The address is printed, but the ink should match that on Stacy's desk. He had a brass stamp dispenser, and a microscopic examination might prove that this particular strip of stamps came from that dispenser." He swallowed and said: "But let's open it and see."

He walked over to Elinor Stacy and put the package gently on her knees. He stepped back, dark face set as her eyes held his.

"Go ahead, Mrs. Stacy," he said. "It's addressed to you."

Jerome, his tanned face all humps and wrinkles, was watching her and now, his voice soft and touched with awe, he said, speaking to Murdock but not shifting his gaze:

"She mailed the package to herself in care of my office. You're saying now that Elinor killed her husband."

Murdock made no reply. He was intent on the woman, seeing the tightness begin to work on her face as the color fled. She moistened her lips, but her fingers were steady as they plucked at the string. She was still watching him and he understood beyond all doubt that the intelligence they reflected was genuine. Bitterness and frustration were working in their blue depths now, but there was no sign of defeat.

"You seem very sure of yourself, Mr. Murdock," she said, her quiet voice reflecting no emotion.

Murdock waited, saying nothing.

"Very sure," she said.

The string came loose in her fingers and as he watched them Murdock realized that her hands were slender and well-shaped, like her ankles.

"Do you think," she said, her glance dropping to the package, "that it would be possible for me to have mailed this package *after* someone else had killed Ralph?"

Murdock was in no mood to answer. Again he felt the tension stirring in him, and a stiffness was growing in the backs of his legs. He shifted his weight to give his muscles relief, aware that Jerome was sitting on the edge of his chair, hearing the sound of his breathing in that moment before he spoke.

"Just a minute, Murdock," he said. "You're saying that Elinor made up this package the night her husband was murdered, using a box, paper, and string that were there. Why should she do that? If there was something she wanted, why didn't she just take it with her?"

"Because she is too smart for that," Murdock said, giving him a quick glance. "She's a very intelligent woman and she must have known that when the murder was discovered, especially when the police knew there was a divorce pending and a blonde in the picture, she would be immediately under suspicion."

"Oh," said Jerome without conviction.

"She had to assume that this place might be searched —which it was—and she didn't dare take a chance. She had to get that package out of Stacy's place and she couldn't bring it here."

"So she mailed it."

"In care of your office," Murdock said, "because for all she knew it might have been delivered here the following day—yesterday, which might not be safe if the police were still watching her. But it would be a simple matter for her to leave the package in your office as long as she wanted to. All she had to do was phone you and casually mention that a package might come for her and would you hold it."

"She did phone me," Jerome said. "And then a little while ago I thought you were her lawyer and you asked me to bring it here—" He let the sentence dangle and tried again, his gaze bleak. "You were awfully damned sure I'd bring it, weren't you?"

"I thought you would if I phrased the request properly."

"Because you had an idea there was anything between Elinor and me?"

"Bacon considered the possibility," Murdock said. "But not me. Not after I'd met your wife." He shook his head. "Let's just say I thought you'd bring it because you're a gentleman. A woman employee of yours is in trouble, a simple request is made—as a personal favor. You're not suspicious, so why shouldn't you bring the package? Anyway, it was a chance I had to take."

Jerome no longer seemed to be listening, but his mouth remained partly open as he regarded the woman with an odd, incredulous look, as though he understood the logic of Murdock's premise but still did not believe this thing had happened.

Elinor Stacy had removed the paper. For a second or so her fingers rested quietly on the box top, the tightness in her face showing white at the cheekbones but her gaze narrowed and steady in her inspection of Murdock.

"You seem to know a great deal about this box," she said. "Perhaps you also know what's in it."

"Money, probably," Murdock said. "Cash."

"Yes."

She lifted the crushed cardboard of the cover and dropped it. A twenty-dollar and a fifty-dollar bill came with it and fluttered to the floor. The box was filled with other bills and on the top was a small nickel-plated revolver, which was instantly in her hand.

"Also this," she said and pointed it at Murdock. "Had you forgotten that the police didn't find the gun? . . . Sit down, Mr. Murdock," she said. "Back there in that chair where you were before."

23

THE FIRST thought that came to Kent Murdock as he looked down the muzzle of that little gun and the silence struck at the room was that a man couldn't think of everything. In his concentration on the probable accuracy of his premise he had completely forgotten about the missing gun. Now the thought of his carelessness disgusted him even as the sight of the revolver shocked him. He was not afraid, but the sense of shock remained stark and disturbing and he backed up as directed until he could ease himself into the rocker.

It was Jerome who broke the silence. He exhaled suddenly, a quick and noisy sound, and started to get out of the chair. Before he could quite make it the gun shifted to cover him.

"You stay there too, Mr. Jerome," the woman said.

"There's no reason why you should get hurt if you'll be sensible."

"Then you did kill your husband."

"Yes," she said simply. "I didn't go there to do it, but it happened."

"Because you were jealous and didn't want him to—"

"No," she interrupted, corroborating an impression that had come to Murdock the first night. "I haven't been jealous of Ralph for years."

"He was going to run away with the profits," Murdock said. "And you wanted your share."

"I suppose that would be one way of putting it."

Murdock settled back. He tried not to look at the gun. He tried to keep his attention on the pale, immobile face that no longer seemed so plain. Things were happening behind the intelligent eyes, but he could not guess what they were or what sort of plan was growing in her brain. He remembered his call to Police Headquarters and, while he knew Lieutenant Bacon would be around, he could not tell when. Because time now seemed the most important thing of all he began to talk, quietly and with a politeness that sounded unconcerned.

"You found out Ralph had cleaned out the safe-deposit box," he said. "When he stalled your lawyer you went down to the bank. You didn't have a key, but the box was in your name too and you could inquire, and you found out the truth. . . . You knew he had been black-mailing," he said when there was no denial. "You knew there must be plenty of money."

"I thought there must be." She leaned down, the re-volver steady in her hand, to recover the two bills which had slipped to the floor. Working then with her sense of touch, she put them in the box and covered it. She ar-ranged it beside her and said: "It was even more than I thought—twenty-eight thousand dollars."

"A lot of money."

"Particularly when you've had as little as I had with Ralph. I worked in Chicago. In Buffalo and here—until this year—I didn't, and aside from food and rent money I was lucky to get enough to buy a new dress a year."

"You found out the box was clean and you were afraid he was going to leave town with what was in it."

"It wasn't so much his leaving town," she said. "He could have put it away somewhere so I couldn't find it. I didn't even know how much it was, so how could my lawyer make any claim? Ralph would just deny he had any extra money and make us prove he did."

"You went to his place with that gun," Murdock said.

"But not to kill him."

"You had the gun when those two hoodlums came to search the darkroom."

"In my handbag." She paused, her lashes drooping in her intentness. "But how did you know I had made the package?"

"I didn't," Murdock said, "until this morning. When I began to think it over it was the only assumption I could find that seemed to fit the probabilities."

"The first night you noticed the box and paper were missing, but you didn't do anything about it until this morning," she said, as though wanting to be sure she had the matter straight. "What happened this morning?"

Murdock was glad to have the opportunity to prolong the conversation. He said he wanted a cigarette and was careful not to alarm her when he took it out and lit it.

"Nancy Larkin came to see me," he said. "She kept insisting Jack Frost wasn't guilty. She repeated the things she had told Bacon the first night about her warning Ralph. But she added one more thing. Her original story was that she phoned Ralph's place and got no answer and later tried it again—when I was there—and he came to see her. But she forgot about one other call she made."

He hesitated again to be sure his meaning was clear.

"She said she phoned Ralph and got no answer, and she was scared and a little desperate, so on the off chance that he might have stopped here to see you, she phoned here. There was no answer."

Elinor Stacy's lids opened and all that native intelligence was there and Murdock knew she had the answer even as he put it into words.

"You told Lieutenant Bacon there had been just one phone call here after you left your husband's place, but that you didn't answer it. That was a lie."

"Oh?" she said, her tone challenging.

"You weren't even here when the phone rang. If you had been you would also have heard Nancy's call just a very few mintues earlier and mentioned it. Your story to Bacon, about washing your face and not bothering to answer the call that your husband made, was clever enough, but it wasn't the truth."

He pointed his cigarette at her and said: "You didn't answer that call—or Nancy's a bit earlier—because you weren't here. *Yet you knew Ralph had called*. I say the only way this could happen was that you were at his apartment all the time and heard him make the call from that end."

She did not challenge him this time. A new wariness was showing in her eyes now, a new nervousness was working on her hands. She glanced at Jerome, then back at Murdock, and he went ahead quickly, expanding his theory in the hope of holding her interest.

"I'll have to guess about the rest of it," he said, "but you can stop me if I'm wrong. . . . You did not leave the other apartment after that blond hoodlum knocked you out," he said when she made no reply.

"You had come to settle things with your husband and after what happened you were probably more determined than ever to see it through. You were hurt and angry, and I say you sat down to wait for Ralph, deter-

mined to stay however long you had to stay. You were
there when someone took two shots at Ralph's car and
you must have heard them. You probably went to the
window to see what had happened, and you saw Ralph
had me with him, so you ducked into the back bedroom
because you couldn't settle anything until you had him
alone."

He swallowed and said: "You heard him say he was
going to phone you, heard him dial—and you were smart
enough to remember that call later on and have a proper
explanation for Bacon. You heard the phone ring—that
was Nancy—and you heard Ralph say he was going out
and for me to stick around. You know about the girl
who came with a gun of her own to look for a negative."
He glanced at Jerome, whose mouth was still open and
who seemed not to have moved. This, he knew, could
mean nothing to Jerome, but he did not want to take
the time to digress and explain things, so he said:

"The girl tried Ralph's closet and it was locked. In
the back bedroom the closet door was ajar, but she didn't
bother to open it. If she had you could have thought of
an explanation and no harm done; but she didn't look
and you were still safe and so you probably know all
about Vivian Jerome. . . . I left," he said. "Then Ralph
came back. What happened between them I don't know,
but she did leave him five hundred dollars in new bills
before she left. . . . So then you walked out with your
little gun," he said, "and told Ralph what you wanted."

"He had the envelope and the money in his hand," she
said dully. "He put it in his pocket and then he laughed
at me when I told him I knew about the safe-deposit
box. So I took out the gun and it scared him, just as I
knew it would. I made him go to his bedroom and unlock
the closet, and I saw the briefcase and made him open
that too."

Her glance slid past him then and there was great

distance in it. "I had no idea there was so much," she said, her voice little more than a whisper. "I didn't expect it at all. I was going to take it and keep it until I could talk to my lawyer. I was entitled to half and that's all I wanted, but Ralph must have thought he was going to lose it all. He grabbed at the gun and I pulled the trigger."

She stopped to wet her lips and the silence expanded and then she said: "I don't know what happened then. I just kept pulling the trigger."

Murdock let his breath out and put his cigarette butt away. He glanced again at Jerome. "Did it occur to you," he said to the woman, "that you would have inherited that money if you had left it there?"

"Oh, yes," she said. "That was what I was afraid of. As you said, I knew I would be suspected, and if the money was found the police would say I knew about it, that the money was my motive."

"Smart," Murdock thought. "Very smart."

"You thought of everything," he said aloud. "You didn't make any mistakes. You had some good luck and it was the bad luck that licked you. The phone call Nancy Larkin forgot to mention—and a guy named Martin Epps."

He considered Randolph Jerome as his mind went on.

"You came down when Epps phoned you from the drugstore," he said. "Then what?"

"Just as I told you," Jerome said huskily. "My wife had gone—at least, that is what Epps told me—and I left too."

"He stayed."

"Yes."

"And then"—Murdock looked back at Elinor Stacy—"you came out with your package. Soon after that Jack Frost came, and if he went up and found Ralph, as I think he did, he probably came out four times as fast as he went in. . . . Epps didn't follow you home, did he?"

"No. He came the next day. He knew Ralph was married and separated and it wasn't hard to find me." Her mouth tightened, as though at the memory, and a hard, bright glitter filmed her eyes. "I gave him the five hundred dollars I'd taken from Ralph's pocket. I had to. He wanted to know about the package. He said the five hundred wasn't enough for the risk he was taking.

"I hated him," she said, her tone suddenly taut and virulent, "with his dirty hands and his crude insinuations. But I knew I had to offer him more. I told him I would but that I couldn't get the cash for a day or two."

"Last night you went to see him," Murdock said.

"He phoned me. He said the police might start to crowd him and he wanted to see me."

"Did you go in the back way?"

"Why, no," she said, as though she found the thought surprising.

Murdock thought of the two detectives who had been waiting out front and understood once more the fickleness of luck. For the detectives were looking only for Epps. They had seen Elinor Stacy enter the building, but they had no interest in women and had no doubt classified her as a customer of the loan company. She had gone to see Epps and done what she had to do, and then she had walked out. It was as simple as that.

The thought of this brought Jack Frost to mind and he wondered if Frost had used the back door and if he had come by appointment.

"You didn't know that Jack Frost also came, that you couldn't have missed him by more than a minute or two."

"No."

"You didn't have a gun that time either, did you?"

"I didn't have anything. I did not dare not go, so I went. He was just the same: avaricious and leering and insulting. I think he expected me to offer him everything I had taken from Ralph, but what he said was that he didn't think he could afford to take any more chances. He said he was going to have to tell the police the truth."

She paused, her voice hushed. "But still he wasn't alarmed. I asked him to wait another day until I could get the money, but I knew then that his word would mean nothing. I knew I couldn't trust him. There was a heavy glass paperweight on the desk and some papers, and I knocked the papers off and he stooped to pick them up. I hit him. I knew I was going to. It didn't seem to matter any more, because I wasn't the same person I was before"—she faltered—"before I shot Ralph."

The thought was well put and Murdock knew exactly what she meant. What surprised him was that he could consider her neither with pity nor distaste. Her outward matter-of-factness had set up a like reaction inside him and this new objectivity was reflected in his voice.

"You found his gun," he said, "and so you didn't have to keep hitting him with the paperweight. I guess it was you who arranged for Epps to search this place yesterday, wasn't it?"

Her silence was enough and he said: "You had to make a deal with him. You knew Bacon suspected you and you wanted the best red herring you could find. You thought it all out and you did extremely well, once you remembered the negatives Ralph had in the bookcase. You knew he'd been blackmailing people."

"I've already said I did," she said, a snap in her voice and a new glint in her eyes.

"And I was the guy to give them to. Old Murdock would know what to do," he continued bluntly. "Murdock would check back and find out what Ralph had been doing. Murdock would eventually tell the police and then the pressure would be off you while they looked for blackmail motives elsewhere. . . . Very neat," he said, "that idea of calling me at the *Courier* and getting me to come over and walk you here so we could discover the place had been ransacked. You made Epps promise to help you to that extent."

"I had to," she said. "I had to make it look as though someone was still looking for those negatives."

Murdock laughed shortly, an unpleasant sound. "And as a matter of fact, someone was—Joe Calenda. I guess you sent Epps to Nancy Larkin's to make the plant that much better."

"He hit her because he had to," she said. "She walked in on him."

"Okay." Murdock leaned forward, watching Jerome from the corner of his eye. "I think you might have made it if it hadn't been for Epps. You killed him deliberately —though I'm not sure the State can prove its case—but for your husband, deliberate or not, you'll have to pay up. Maybe a good lawyer might battle it out to first-degree manslaughter. That gun and the money are all the district attorney will need."

He started to rise and she lifted the gun. "Stay where you are."

"Elinor!" Jerome came to his feet in spite of her threat, his face shining with perspiration. "Think what you're doing. You can't possibly get away now."

"I can try."

"But where will you go?"

"I don't know, but I'd like to try." She was directing her words to him now, though she still watched Murdock. "You're a sensible man. I don't want to shoot unless I have to—I've had enough shooting—but I want you to take Mr. Murdock into the bathroom. I can lock it from the outside. I think it might give me a few minutes' start."

"But—"

She shook her head as though to shut out the argument, her mouth a thin red slash in the otherwise chalky face.

"Do as I say." She tapped the box. "I think I've earned this now and I'd like a chance to spend some of it."

"You'd better save some of it for a lawyer," Jerome said stiffly.

"Maybe I won't need a lawyer."

Murdock understood how it was. Further argument could only be futile with the woman's present state of mind, so he stood up and again she threatened him with the revolver.

"I mean it," she said, her voice tight with strain. "I'll shoot."

"No." Murdock shook his head wearily.

"What do you mean? That I'm afraid?"

"Not that," Murdock said. "Just that I think you did too much shooting the first night. Did you take some extra bullets with you?"

"What?"

"I doubt it," he said, answering himself. "But you've forgotten you shot Ralph six times. That's all that revolver holds; I can tell that from here."

For an instant then as Murdock took his first step her face seemed to fall apart as the panic struck at her. She glanced down at the gun, her eyes suddenly horrified. She glanced up at Murdock's approaching figure; then yanked at the trigger.

Even then she would not admit defeat. When the hammer clicked harmlessly she threw it at him and snatched at the box. Murdock had to duck and then it was too late to cut her off as she wheeled swiftly away from the couch and ran to the open door of the bedroom.

Murdock hit it a second after the lock clicked. He felt Jerome, who was a step behind, bounce off him. He turned and they stood that way, breathing hard, staring at each other with unseeing eyes.

Murdock put his ear to the panel and then straightened, aware now that his hands were trembling and wet at the palms. He got out a handkerchief and wiped them, wiped his face when he discovered it was also damp.

"It's all right," he said. "She can't get out and Bacon should be here any minute."

Even as he spoke he could hear the distant wail of a siren and with it came some other sound, faint and indefinable, from inside the room. He listened again and now he heard still another sound more urgent than the others, a sharply phrased call which came not from the room but from somewhere outside the apartment.

"What was that?" Jerome had stiffened, his head swiveling to stare at the windows.

He started for them, Murdock at his side.

Down on the street someone hit the siren again and now they heard the shout, muted but distinct, which came again from outside the building. A man's voice, it carried the same strident inflection they had heard before, and when they opened the window they knew why.

Elinor Stacy's apartment was at the rear, overlooking an alley. Both the living-room and bedroom windows faced in this direction and as they crowded into the opening they saw first the man leaning stiff-armed from the window one flight below and across the alley. A baldheaded man in a T-shirt, he looked up as he heard their window, his face still stiff with shock.

"Yelled at her," he cried. "I told her not to jump."

They glanced down then as the wail of the siren faded into silence. Five floors below them and sprawled flat on the rough paving like a broken doll, the woman who had been Elinor Stacy lay crushed and unmoving.

Close by was a lopsided cardboard box, and spilling from it were what looked like rectangular slips of paper that stirred and skittered in the faint breeze. From that height the contents of the box defied identification; certainly the man across the way could not have recognized those slips as money. Only Murdock and Jerome knew. Only they could guess that in her obsession to hold this wealth that had for so long been denied her, Elinor Stacy had tried to cling to it even in death.

"I tried," the man said. "But she didn't even look at me."

Murdock backed away, fighting against his sudden nausea. He swallowed quickly and found his mouth and throat dry. For a moment he had time to wonder whether the sound of that siren had precipitated the act or whether what was left of the woman's mind had prompted her to seek the easy way out. Then he knew it could not matter and gave his attention to Jerome's quiet cursing as he asked: wasn't there, for God's sake, a drink in the place?

Murdock said there should be something in the kitchen, and then he went over to the telephone. His fingers still shook as he dialed the familiar number, and then, before the connection was made, a thought came to him that, for Murdock, was a very curious one indeed.

For suddenly he discovered he was glad he did not have his camera with him. A picture would be taken shortly, and the *Courier* would carry that picture in the morning, but this time it would be someone else who pressed the shutter, not Murdock.

He said what he had to say to the city editor and then, hearing the elevator stop at that floor, he said he would have to call back. He was crossing to the door when the pounding came, and in that second or two before he opened it to admit Bacon he thought of something else. For in his effort to blot out the memory of the past few minutes his mind slid off on a tangent and he remembered Betty Hargrove's invitation. The thought of this brought again a brief anticipatory glow and he knew it would be something to think about during the next few hours when he would be busy with other things. But there should be time. With luck he would be at her place at seven. On the dot.

A NOTE ON THE TYPE

The text of this book is set in Caledonia, a Linotype face designed by W. A. Dwiggins, the man responsible for so much that is good in contemporary book design and typography. Caledonia belongs to the family of printing types called "modern face" by printers—a term used to mark the change in style of type-letters that occurred about 1800. It has all the hardworking feet-on-the-ground qualities of the Scotch Modern face plus the liveliness and grace that is integral in every Dwiggins "product" whether it be a simple catalogue cover or an almost human puppet.